Ivy's Dilemma

a novel by Reign

Dreams Publishing Co.
P.O. Box 4731
Rocky Mount, NC 27803
www.DreamsPublishing.com

ISBN 0-9770936-0-3
1. Religion-Christianity - Christian Life - Family Relationships
2. Family & Relationships-Love & Romance 3. Periodicals-
Literary - African American

First published in the United States September 2005
Library of Congress Control Number (LCCN): 2005929913

Designed in Rocky Mount, North Carolina, by Nicki Angela.
Printed and bound in the United States of America

Dedication

This book is dedicated to my children, Sheena, Calvin Jr., Chanel, Brittney, Brandon and Varonaca. All things are possible to them that believe. Through Christ you have the victory, now!

Acknowledgements

I wish to thank my Father and my God through Christ Jesus who is everything to me. To my mother, Sula Thomas Walker, Just because I love you. To my proofreaders, Hope Phillips and Teresa Rhodes, I thank God for you and your faith in this story and for encouraging me to finish the book. Both of you are jewels. To my reading group, Betty Joyner, Dorothy V. Lamkin, Pam Cofield and Gloria Wheeler. I will forever be grateful to each of you. To my illustrator, Larry Russell, Thank you for allowing your art to grace this cover. To my editor, Jeannette Cezanne, (Dr. J.), you have been a gift from God. To my friend, Janice Sims, thank you for your input and encouragement. To author, Brenda M. Hampton, your advice has been invaluable. To my husband Calvin, thank you my darling for cheering me on and having more faith in me than I had in myself, I love you so much.

2 Corinthians 7:10 For godly sorrow worketh repentance to salvation not to be repented of: but the sorrow of the world worketh death.

Romans 6:23 For the wages of sin is death; but the gift of God is eternal life through Jesus Christ our Lord.

PROLOGUE

He blinked once, and then again. He was tired. Having had no sleep in twenty-four hours was taking its toll. He blinked yet another time, and then rolled down the car window, allowing the cool air to hit his face. It was just a few more miles to the hotel, and he could hear the bed calling his name. When he got there, he promised himself, he would sleep for ten hours straight.

He looked over at his companion. She had reclined her seat and was already asleep. He wiped his eyes and forced them open again, willing himself to stay awake. He needed to get to the hotel, and he needed to get there fast. So he accelerated, bringing the car up to seventy, even though he knew that the speed limit was only forty-five.

He reached over and turned on the radio. Earth, Wind and Fire's *Reasons* was playing, and the song made him think of his wife. He took a deep breath and exhaled slowly.

He had to admit it, the woman sitting next to him was nothing compared to his wife. His wife was equipped with brains and beauty, neither of which this woman possessed in any remarkable way. So why was he running around disrespecting Ivy? The only answer he could come up with was, *because I can.*

He wiped his eyes, blinked, and by the time he opened them – *Oh my God!* – two giant lights were coming right at him. He twisted the steering wheel savagely in an attempt to avoid contact with the vehicle in front of him, but the lights just followed his move.

Someone was screaming his name. He slammed on the brakes, making the tires squeal, and suddenly the car was spinning completely out of control, spinning for what seemed like forever, in a slow-motion arc, time spinning out along with the car. Finally it flipped, creating sparks as it slid on its side across the asphalt.

When the vehicles collided, there was nothing that could be done to stop the metal from crushing the dashboard and making contact with the occupants inside.

He heard the sirens, as well as the crying and screaming. "Get him out, please get him out," said a familiar voice. "Hold on, baby." Why couldn't he move? He opened his eyes and tried to focus on what was in front of him.

He needed to free himself from the mangled car. When he tried to move his hands, he could see why he was immobile. There was crushed metal pressed to his chest, pinning him to the seat of the car. He was trying to tell them to get the stuff off of him, but he couldn't speak. He felt excruciating pain all over his body each time someone tried to pull him from the wreckage. *Don't. Stop.* Nothing was coming from his lips. He needed them to stop trying to move him. If everyone would just calm down, he could get his bearings and let them know what was needed to be done to get him out of this mess.

Smoke. He could feel heat. *Oh no, the car is about to explode*, he thought. Water was drenching his face and there was a bunch of people out there doing only God knows what. Something wasn't right. He was gasping for breath. He needed to tell them the metal on his chest was making it hard to take in air. He wanted to move himself, but his legs wouldn't cooperate.

He opened his mouth to speak and blood poured out instead of words.

Chapter One

Ivy Jones-Miller sat on the side of her bed. In one hand she held a picture of her husband of eleven years; in the other, a copy of the documents filing for a divorce from him.

She had to admit the reality: she still loved Raymond Terrell Miller. He had been part of her life since she was ten years old. For sixteen years, their families lived next door to each other. Both families had been members of the Cathedral Of Faith Christian Center in Camden, New Jersey, where Ivy's grandfather was founder and pastor. They had grown up together. And she honestly couldn't imagine what her life was going to be like without him in it.

With tears streaming down her cheeks, she released the documents and watched as they slipped down to land near her feet on the plush carpeted floor. Hugging the photograph to her breast, she willed herself to accept that this was the end of her life with Ray.

The feeling had to be worse than death itself.

What she was realizing was that all the material possessions she and Ray had accumulated meant nothing if he was not here to share them with her. She had been willing to give up this tremendous house with its breathtaking view of the lake, a view she had enjoyed for many years from the bay window in the morning kitchen. The Bentley, the Mercedes, and every piece of jewelry she owned – she would have relinquished it all, gladly, just to have him with her again.

Yes, just to have Ray in her arms and back in her life the way it used to be, she would be willing to live like a vagabond.

And here was the ultimate irony, even though she was willing to give up everything, he still didn't want her anymore. He had told her, his voice flat and distant, to file for a divorce; and since that day he hadn't slept in their home.

Ivy looked over at numerous pictures of Ray and herself that were sitting on her dresser. She walked over to them and stared at each, one by one. "I hate that I ever met you," she said out loud as she looked intently at his image. She picked up the heavy gold-framed photograph and after staring at it a few moments more, she pitched it against the wall on the opposite side of the room. She watched as the glass shattered against the wall, falling onto the carpet.

She turned her attention back to the other photos. "I hate you," she repeated. The three words came from her lips; but in her heart, that was far from the truth. "Oh, God, what am I going to do?" She crumpled to the floor. The truth was she wanted to hate him. She needed to hate him. It was too hard to accept, otherwise.

After a few minutes of self-pity, the anger surged back. She stood up and grabbed a crystal-framed photograph of Ray in his Redskins uniform. She dropped it to the floor and began to stomp on it, over and over again. Each time her foot smashed onto the picture she said a word. "I," stomp, "hate," stomp, "you," chanting it over and over again, trying her best to make a lie the truth so the pain in her heart would go away. "Damn you, Ray. I gave you the best of me. I gave you all of me. I'm the mother of your children. How could you be so cruel?"

She cried until she was spent. Then as the tears began to subside, Ivy stood and swung her arm over the dresser, flinging everything on it to the floor.

"What am I going to do?" She murmured the words out loud. "How am I going to live without him?"

She hadn't told a soul that Ray had left her. Perhaps telling someone would make her face the fact that it was truly over. Her guess was that everyone would be shocked, especially when they found out that she and Ray were divorcing. She came from a Christian family that did not divorce.

How was she going to explain this to her family? She was a minister's daughter. Her family believed in *until death do you part* – and so did she: it would have been that way, too, if she had her way.

But the choice was out of her hands. *It's in God's hands now*, she thought. She would have to stop all this crying and be strong and face the fact that she had done all she could to save this marriage. The final papers were signed and had been delivered to the attorney; it was time to inform the people closest to her. Maybe after she opened up and shared her grief with the people who really cared about her, she could begin the healing process, begin to become whole again.

First she needed to tell their children. Ray Jr. the oldest, was nine, Solomon, was five, and the twin girls, Tamara and Terra, were three. Ivy wiped the tears from her eyes with the back of her hand, took a deep breath and commanded herself to get it together.

It was time that she accepted that Ray had left her and his entire family a long time ago, long before he voiced his desire for a divorce. Filing the paperwork only made it official.

Ivy knew that she didn't need to blame herself, at least not entirely: there was enough blame to go around. Other women. Drugs. It has been nearly two years since Ray's last attempt to rid his life of the drugs. After failing to complete three different programs at three different facilities, her father, the Reverend James Jones, had recommended the Faith and Hope Drug and Alcohol Rehabilitation Center. Reverend Jones was now the pastor of Cathedral Of Faith Christian Center and he knew people who had attended the Center; he had suggested this facility because of the highly successful completion rate of their clients. Through his work with the inner-city youth at the Ray Miller Youth Center, he had sent many others through the drug program offered at Faith and Hope.

Nevertheless, Ray had yet again failed to finish the program.

How could all this have happened right under Ivy's nose? How could she not have recognized the warnings? All the signs had been there, right in front of her. Had she been in denial? Or had she simply been deaf to anything that threatened her marriage, her happiness? When they had first started out, she would never have thought in a million years that Ray would be stupid enough to get himself hooked on any drug, especially one as addictive and harmful as heroin.

She put her head back on her pillow, closing her eyes. She was torturing herself, she knew, but she couldn't help but think back, to remember a time when life had been wonderful. Yes, there had been a lot of good times with Ray. They had had the leading roles in their sixth-grade play at Morgan Village Middle School. She remembered their first real slow dance at the seventh-grade spring festival, the sophomore cotillion where they shared their first real kiss, and the junior and senior proms where they first confessed their love for each other.

The fondest memory of all was the senior class trip to Florida. That was when Ray had told her he would not go away to college without her.

Ray had come to the room that she shared with three other girls, telling her he needed to talk. It was early Sunday morning, and in the blistering heat of the Florida sun, Ivy and Ray walked hand in hand toward the banana tree located on the side of the hotel where the seniors were staying. It was the first time they were alone since they arrived two days before. Ray had with him a large beach towel and he spread it on the ground under the tree.

Ivy leaned her head against Ray's arm. "You are a real romantic, you know that," she said to him.

"Well, I aim to please," he answered with *that smile*, the smile that made her insides melt, and then he kissed her on the forehead. "But I really need to talk to you about us."

Ivy looked up into his eyes. She could tell he was serious. "What?"

"I love you, Ivy," he said softly.

"I know, and I love you too," she answered, still a little puzzled.

His dark eyes held unimaginable depths. "I don't want to go to school without you."

Ivy made light of it. Always sensible, even back then. "Ray, you're going to Delaware, and I'm going to Rutgers. It's not like we're a thousand miles away from each other. We'll see each other on weekends and maybe even some weekdays. We'll be about fifty miles from each other!"

"I don't care, fifty miles might as well be five thousand," he said. His voice was gentle and steady. "I want you in my room and in my bed every night."

"Oh, so it's about *that* again," Ivy said teasingly. *The eternal issue with all young men*, she thought.

He wasn't deterred by her tone. "Yeah, it's about me wanting you, Ivy. Now, and forever."

She struggled to sit up and looked directly at him. If he wanted honesty, she'd give him honesty. "Ray, it's about sex, and you know it. I'm not marrying you just so we can sleep together!"

"Why would I marry you just to sleep with you? I could sleep with any girl I want! It's not about sex. It's about me loving you and not wanting to be separated from you."

"Ray…"

"Listen, Ivy. We've been together since we were kids. I know how I feel about you and I see how other guys look at you."

"Ray…"

"Let me finish, Ivy." His voice was stronger now. He paused and took both her hands in his. "I watch other guys checking you out and just the mere thought of them being with you in any kind of way makes me sick to my stomach."

"I love you, Ray!" she protested. "I would never …"

He put his finger over her lips to stop her words. "Marry me, Ivy." She stared at him. When he dropped his head, placing it on her shoulder, he whispered against her ear, "Please."

As his breath caressed her ear, Ivy shivered and took a deep intake of air to stabilize herself. Using the palm of her hand, she lifted Ray's head so she could look into his eyes. She kissed his lips and they smiled at each other. Then Ivy asked, "Can I say something now?"

"Not if you're gonna tell me no," He was pouting like a child.

"I love you. How can I say no?"

Ray brightened immediately. "You mean that?" There was excitement in his voice.

"Of course I do. You know I love you and I want to marry you. But not now, Ray." His shoulders slumped. "Honey, think about it. You know my parents won't approve of their only daughter marrying. Especially before going to college. And what about your folks? Do you really want to take on our parents? We'll need them to help support us while we're in school. I don't want to fight with them." Ivy paused for a few moments. "Look, we'll have a four-year engagement, and I promise I won't date other guys."

Ray wanted them to marry before the semester began. Both families were against the idea, though, and he knew it. He let Ivy persuade him to wait.

Or so she thought.

A few weeks later, with the families gathered together for the traditional Fourth of July barbeque, Ray and Ivy announced their plan to be married.

Their wedding was that August, one week before Ray entered Delaware State University on a full football scholarship – with Ivy attending the same school too. They were only eighteen and nineteen years old.

It was a beautiful memory. It said everything about what they had been to each other. Or maybe it just said that they had been very, very young.

Now Ivy looked at the third finger on her left hand. Her wedding and engagement rings were gone. She had pawned them last week to pay the water and sewer bills, and to put some food in the refrigerator. The owner of the pawnshop told her she had thirty days to redeem them; but as she walked away, she knew the rings were lost forever.

The ringing of the telephone interrupted her thoughts. "Hello?"

"Hey, sweetie, it's me," Ivy recognized her mother's voice. "Just checking in. Do you have everything you need for your get-together this weekend with the girls?"

Ivy's throat constricted. "Well," she hesitated, "I was actually thinking that I should maybe cancel, because…"

"You aren't canceling anything," her mother said crisply before Ivy could finish her excuse. "I told you to have the girls over this weekend because right now you need to be around your friends. I know you've been depressed, and I think this will be good medicine for whatever's ailing you."

"Yes, Mama, I know you're right, and yes, I have everything. I do believe you made sure of that."

"Good. Well, now, I called you for another reason, what was it? Oh, yeah, I called to tell you that I talked to Jade. She's decided to come after all, and she's bringing her son with her."

"Really!" Ivy exclaimed, interested despite her own heartache. "It's about time she brings the little crumb-snatcher here so we can see him! What did you do, threaten her life to make her change her mind?"

"I didn't have to do anything. She was trying to call you earlier this morning, and when she couldn't reach you she called me. I tried to call you myself. Where have you been all morning?"

"I was with my attorney." Just thinking about why she was with her attorney made her eyes fill with water. *I won't cry*, she told herself; *I won't break down.*

"Oooh," was all her mother said. The atmosphere was still for a moment. Ivy knew that if she didn't volunteer an explanation for the remark she'd just made to her mother, she would hang up the telephone without one. She took a deep breath. "I filed for a divorce on Tuesday, Mama, and I had some other papers I had to sign and go over this morning before he takes them to the courthouse."

"Oh, Ivy, sweetie, I'm so sorry it's come to that." Patricia Jones was sympathy itself. No condemnation there, Ivy thought gratefully. Thank you, God. Thank you, Mama.

"I am, too. But I'm okay, Mama," Ivy said. It was a lie, but what else could she do? Her mother knew her well, and would know that she was lying, and neither of them had to talk about it.

Ivy's mother was wise beyond her fifty years. She was small in size but huge at heart, meek and humble. Her inner beauty radiated clear through to her personality.

"Well, now I *know* that this weekend is the right thing to do. I'm happy that you're going to be spending it with your friends."

"Thanks, Mama. And thank you for footing the bill, 'cause I'm sure you know I can't afford it." She sat back down on the edge of her bed. The one that, once, she had shared with her husband. *Don't think about that. Think about something else.* "I'm really glad to know that Jade is coming," she said. "I can't believe she's bringing the baby."

She was too restless to stay still, sitting there. She stood up again, carrying the cordless phone with her, idly picking up the papers she had scattered earlier, straightening them, putting them in the nightstand drawer. Better to do something aimless than to do nothing at all.

Her mother was still talking. "I told her I was keeping all the children so you girls could just relax and have a good time. Oh, by the way, I picked up a case of sparkling apple cider for you all, and a few other things. I'll bring them when I pick up the kids."

"Mama, I love you."

"I know you do. I'm a little crazy about you, too."

Both women were laughing as they hung up the phone.

* * *

Ray had wanted Ivy to donate as much time as she could to the center that had been named for him. It was at his insistence that she had had a housekeeper for eight years. As of three months ago, though, she'd become reacquainted with cleaning her own house.

She changed into a jogging suit, pulled her waist-length hair into a ponytail, and spent the next few hours doing just that. She finished changing the last set of linens in the bedroom and was disconnecting the central vacuum cleaner hose from the wall when she heard the doorbell ring. As she went to answer the door, it hit her that she was actually looking forward to this weekend.

She and her friends hadn't all been together in more than two years.

Squinting through the peephole, she saw Jade standing on the porch, holding what could only be her son. Ivy flung open the door, stood back, and looked at this woman who had been her friend for over fifteen years. "Jade, girl, I'm so glad you changed your mind and came! Get inside, you're letting the heat out." Ivy's smile shone across her face. She hugged Jade and the baby at the same time.

"I came here to hide out for a few days," Jade admitted honestly, following her friend into the house.

Jade and Ivy had met when Jade's family moved from North Carolina to New Jersey, into the house on the corner of the street where Ivy lived. The girls were both fifteen years old, yet Jade was two grades behind students her age. Ivy soon found out that being two grades behind had nothing to do with her new friend's intelligence. Jade was extremely smart, so smart that she tutored other kids in the neighborhood who were much older than she. She even helped Ray pass the math portion of the SATs.

She was street-wise, too. Jade hardly ever smiled when they first met. She put up a good front, always acting hard and tough; but her kind-heartedness shone through her tough-girl act in spite of herself. She claimed that she tutored for the income, but Ivy had seen how hard her friend worked with other kids, how much she wanted them to succeed.

Jade never talked about her past: that subject was taboo, and she deflected any attempts on Ivy's part to get her to discuss her years before she moved to New Jersey. Jade told her over and over again to stop asking: "I had no life before I moved to New Jersey."

There was a secretive side to Jade, a side that Ivy didn't know if she'd ever be able to access, ever be able to understand. And the secrets weren't all in the distant past, either, Ivy realized now as she held out her arms. "Give me that baby! Let me take a good look at my godson." Ivy took the child from Jade's arms. "Dang, I think I woke him."

"It's okay, he needs to wake up. He slept for most of the trip here." Jade stretched her arms. "That boy is getting heavy. Hey, am I the first to arrive?" Jade walked ahead of Ivy into the living room. Stopping abruptly, she asked, "Where's the piano?"

Ivy ignored her friend's question, hefting the sleepy baby automatically on top her hip. "Come on, let's go to the family room, it's more comfortable there. I haven't seen my godson since he was born. How old is he now?"

"Eighteen months. He'll be two in April." Jade took off her coat and laid it on a chair.

Ivy sat the baby on her lap, and looked at her friend. "You look good, girl! And I love your curly hairstyle." Jade giggled and ran her fingers through her golden brown tresses. Ivy shook her head. "I won't be calling you plain Jade anymore, look at you! You've even arched your eyebrows, haven't you? I like it, girl. It gives those beautiful golden brown eyes more definition."

"Well, thank you, Ivy, you're not looking bad yourself." She ignored the running pants and looked down at Ivy's bare feet. "I see you're still allergic to shoes."

"Girl, you know my toes love to be free." She jiggled the baby and, looking up, noticed something a trick of the light had hidden from her before. "What happened to your face?"

Jade placed her hand over the bruised area. "Oh, it's nothing. It'll be gone by tomorrow." She sat down, put her hands together, and began twisting the ring on her finger, a sure sign that she was nervous about something.

Ivy almost pursued the issue, but she stayed quiet, telling herself that she had all weekend to find out what was going on with her friend and Jade usually needed to bring things up in her own way, in her own time. That tough-girl act again, left over from her childhood. There was no sense in pushing her.

Ivy turned her attention back to the baby. "You have gotten so big, Boo-Boo," she cooed as she sat him on the loveseat next to her and began to remove his snowsuit. Once that task was done, Ivy sat the boy up to take a good look at him and, when she did, he looked up, smiling, showing beautiful dark gray eyes and a head full of jet black curly hair. Ivy couldn't help but be mesmerized by the child's face. As a matter of fact, he was drop-dead gorgeous. "Oh my God," Ivy murmured as the revelation sank in.

She heard Jade say something, but her mind was totally blank as she assessed the child's resemblance to Darrell Parker. She couldn't believe what she was seeing. The boy's eyes were just like Darrell's. His mouth was just like Darrell's. Everything, Ivy thought with sudden understanding, was just like Darrell's.

Jade was saying something else, and she took her son from a stunned Ivy and cradled him to her chest. But Ivy was still lost in her own thoughts.

It was Ivy who had introduced Jade to Darrell when they were only juniors in high school. Darrell was a year ahead of Jade, and the son of Ivy's father's assistant pastor. Darrell was tall and lanky when he was in the eleventh grade. His lightly tanned skin, dark gray eyes, and jet black hair made him stand out from all the other guys, and Jade was smitten. They became lovers during Jade's freshman year at Temple University. He was a sophomore at Rutgers in Camden. After Darrell graduated from college, he began working for an engineering firm in Philadelphia. A year later, Jade too graduated and began working on her Juris Doctor degree at Rutgers in Camden.

Near the end of the second term of her first year of law school, Jade found out she was pregnant. After completing that term, she dropped out of school and abruptly moved to Maryland with the excuse that she couldn't stay because the child was not Darrell's.

Now Ivy blinked hard as she saw Jade's mouth moving, but she could not at first understand a word her friend was saying. "I really tried to tell you," Jade said softly, gently. There was a short pause as she forced air from her nostrils, then sucked at her teeth. "Every time I tried, I just couldn't bring myself to do it."

Ivy now simply sat and looked at her, her mouth open, as if to say something. But it was Jade who spoke. "Now that you've seen him, you don't have to stare at him like he's an alien or something."

Ivy closed her mouth. She couldn't form a word to save her life.

Jade took a deep breath. "Maybe I shouldn't have come, after all."

"Now that's just ridiculous," Ivy said, coming back to life and embarrassed at having made her friend uncomfortable. "Will you please give a woman a chance to recover? Dang." Ivy took the child from Jade's arms. After looking at him again, Ivy said, "You told us that you weren't pregnant by Darrell, that's all. What am I supposed to think? You had this whole line about that was the reason you lied to Darrell and told him that you lost the baby so he wouldn't know you were pregnant with another man's baby. Why did you do that?

"I have my reasons. And right now I'd rather not talk about it," Jade wasn't meeting Ivy's eyes.

"My God, Jade, he looks *just* like Darrell!"

"I know he does, so much so that I should have named him Darrell, but I didn't. His named is Desmond," Jade sighed.

"You don't have to tell me what his name is. I know his name is Desmond, I'm his godmother, remember? I was there when you gave birth to him." Ivy examined his little hand. The resemblance was astonishing. "He looks just like him." Ivy looked over at Jade.

Jade relaxed her shoulders. "I haven't gone home to see my parents in over a year because of it. And the older he gets, the more he looks *just* like Darrell. But for now, do me a favor, Ivy, and don't talk about it, okay? I just want to relax and enjoy this time with you."

Ivy nodded. "Mom picked up my kids about two hours ago. She told me to call her when you got here so she could pick up – little Darrell." Ivy couldn't resist poking fun at her friend. "Never mind. I'll give her a call and then you and I can catch up," she said. "And you can start by giving me a real big hug!"

Chapter Two

Miranda arrived not long after Ivy's mother left with Jade's son.

"Jade!" she screeched in excitement, seeing Jade for the first time in nearly two years. Jade's response was just as delighted. They hugged and kissed each other on the cheek. "You look good, my sister. Look at you," Miranda said as she circled Jade, checking her out fully. "Where is plain Jade and what in the world did you do with her body? Girl, whatcha been doin'? You look fabulous, darling. I can't even tell you've had a baby."

"Well, looks are deceiving, but you don't look bad yourself."

"Girl, I know I don't look bad," she agreed with a smile, twisting one of her natural dreadlocks. "I lost twenty-five pounds, which means I only have thirty more to go to be all that, a bag of chips and a…"

"Shut up, Randi," Ivy told her.

"Don't be mean 'cause you jealous, give me a hug," Miranda said to her cousin, greeting her with a kiss as well. When she released Ivy she stood back and looked at her. "Girl, you're still losin' weight, I'm the one with the extra pounds, not you."

"No, I'm not. I actually gained five pounds."

"Where?" Jade asked sarcastically.

"Oh, it's all in her head. That's why her head's so big." Jade and Miranda laughed.

Ivy walked into the kitchen where she had begun to prepare her favorite spaghetti dinner. As the women followed, they exchanged glances; it wasn't like Ivy to not crack a smile at their jokes.

Miranda and Ivy were cousins. Miranda's father and Ivy's father were identical twins. Four years before, Miranda's father had passed away suddenly after being hospitalized with pneumonia. The cousins were very close, even though Miranda was three years younger than Ivy.

As Miranda walked past the living room, she noticed the baby grand piano was missing, as well as the St. James painting. Nevertheless, as always, the house was beautiful. Miranda had always thought the house could be featured on MTV's "Cribs" show. She leaned lightly against the island in the kitchen. "You know we're just joking with you, Ivy."

Jade sat at the table, nodding. *Something's wrong,* she thought.

Miranda obviously was thinking along the same lines. "Where's the piano, Ivy?" she asked, trying to make her voice sound casual. When no answer came, she looked to Jade, murmuring for her ears only, "What's up with her?" Miranda waited a few moments, then asked, "What's wrong, Ivy? You're not acting like yourself. I know you're not tripping over a fat joke. Normally something like that would have you comin' right back with a line of your own." Ivy was still silent.

Jade shrugged and changed the subject. "When will Sheena be here? I haven't seen her in a zillion moons."

"I've filed for a divorce," Ivy blurted out.

There was a moment of stunned silence. Unable to look at her friends, Ivy kept chopping onions, her movements mechanical. *This is the best time to dice them*, she thought, *because I may need an excuse, just in case I begin crying again.*

Still with her back to her friends, Ivy went on. "That's not all," she said. "Ray hasn't been paying the mortgage and the house is up for foreclosure." Then Ivy turned to see both women looking directly at her. "I signed the final paperwork this morning making my filing official." They were still silent. "Ray and I don't communicate anymore, and he has no respect for me."

Neither woman said anything. Ivy figured they were trying to absorb what she had just told them. "He came to the house about two weeks ago, early in the morning, and it was the first time I'd seen him in over a week. He took a shower, got all dressed up and smelling good. I didn't say a word to him. I guess he expected me to argue with him, but I held my peace. Then I heard a car horn outside and he ran to the door. Do you know I watched my husband from our bedroom window as he and his woman kissed right there in the middle of the street in front of our home?"

Jade gasped.

"Oh, Ivy, no!" Miranda was flabbergasted.

"Yes, they did. Then they got in his car and left." The pain in Ivy's heart shimmered in her voice. "He had the nerve to come back that evening, pack some of his things and tell me to divorce him. And I haven't seen him since."

Miranda felt her own heart beat fast in sympathy. She loved both Ray and Ivy. But Ivy was blood.

Jade could feel the misery as well, but had no words to show Ivy how she felt.

After a moment, Ivy continued. "I sold the piano a month ago, along with some other stuff. I had no choice. Ray isn't paying bills anymore. And when I got home this morning from the attorney's office, the electric company was here to turn off the service. I wrote the man a check to stop him."

"How much money do you have, Ivy?" Miranda asked in a low voice.

Ivy shrugged. "I found a job on Board Street in Philly. I start Monday."

"That wasn't the question. How much money do you have?"

"I'll be okay," Ivy answered.

Miranda raised her voice. "I didn't ask you if you had a job. I didn't ask if you were okay, I asked how much money you have!"

"Randi," Jade's voice was full of caution.

Miranda ignored her. "When I needed money for school it was you who sent it and told me not to tell a soul, and I never did. When I offered to pay it back, you wouldn't take it. You sent me spending money when I didn't even ask for it on a monthly basis. Just tell me why, in the name of God, you didn't call me? Why couldn't you just tell me you needed money?"

Silence.

This time Miranda did shout. "Just tell me why!"

Ivy turned to Miranda in rage and said between clinched teeth, "You don't understand how hard this is for me."

"Maybe I don't, but I do know that I could have helped ease the burden, and you wouldn't even pick up the telephone to call me."

"Miranda's right, Ivy," Jade said suddenly. "You could have called me, too. We are friends, real friends, and you know we're going to do everything within our power to see you through this."

For a moment there was silence. It was broken when Miranda said, with as much compassion as she could put into her voice, "I love you, Ivy."

"That's ditto for me, girlfriend, and you know it," Jade added.

Ivy had to choke back tears. "I know you guys care about me."

Jade put both hands on her hips and said, with a hint of a smile, "We didn't say we just cared about you, you cow, we said we love you."

"Thanks for clearing that up, Jade," Miranda said as she embraced her cousin. "Don't you worry about a thing. Did Bill Hart file the divorce for you?"

Ivy sniffed and tried to marshal her thoughts. "No, he said he can't, because he represents Ray in other matters and there's something about a conflict of interest. I should have known better to ask him in the first place. The man has never cared for me."

"That's crazy, Ivy. You're the one that introduced him to Ray after Sheena recommended him to you. He's been your attorney for years!" Jade was indignant.

Ivy shook her head. "No, actually, he's Ray's attorney. Ray paid him to work for him, not me."

Miranda hesitated, then decided to ask the obvious. "Have you guys tried to work things out?"

"You know I have, but he's gone too far," Ivy said miserably. "He's been to three different drug

rehabilitation centers and he hasn't completed a single program."

Miranda could hear her getting choked up so she changed the conversation. "Look, I need to check on Mama."

"I'm sorry, Randi. I haven't even asked you how Aunt Dee is doing."

"She's about the same. The cancer isn't any better or worse. But the treatments are hard on her."

"Is she back in the hospital?" Jade asked sympathetically.

Miranda shook her head. "No, she's been home since Tuesday. Let me give her a call. I'll use the phone in the family room."

Ivy continued to work at the stove, and Jade thought about her own situation. Compared to what Ivy was going through right now, her own dilemma seemed trivial. Poor Ivy, she mused. From one end of the emotional spectrum to the other.

Ray had played professional football both with the Giants and the Washington Redskins. For nine years he had lived the life of a superstar.

Ray seemed to love his life with Ivy. He certainly provided well for her. He purchased her the house of her dreams, and once the twins came along he ordered a custom van made especially for long travels with his family. He purchased his-and-her Jeeps, a Lexus for him, and a Bentley for her. Life was wonderful. Why did everything have to change?

After making the call to her mother, Miranda sat alone in the family room thinking about Ivy. She shook her head as she thought about Ivy needing to go to work. Now *that* was something her cousin had sworn she'd never do. Ivy had always believed that investing was her job, and she had done well with various stocks, bonds, real estate, and bank CDs. She always said, *let the money work for you, not you work for the money*. Miranda had to find out what Ivy's immediate needs were so they could put a plan in action to help her financially.

At her elbow, the telephone rang suddenly. "Answer the phone, Randi, since you're sitting right by it," Ivy yelled out. Miranda answered, then walked into the kitchen with the cordless phone in hand. She gave it to Ivy. "It's for you. It's somebody at a hospital," she said.

After Ivy walked away to take the call, Jade and Miranda agreed to wait for Sheena to arrive before they decided on how they were going to help Ivy. "Speaking of Sheena, is she still working for the US Department of Education?" Jade asked.

"Yeah," Miranda answered, "she's still there in the attorney's division."

"So… is she dating Mr. Hunk yet?"

Miranda smiled. "By Mr. Hunk, I do believe you mean Jason Jackson?"

"The one and only."

Miranda shrugged lightly. "Yes and no."

Jade raised an eyebrow. "Meaning?"

"They date, but as friends, they bowl together every Thursday night, they eat at Dazz at lease once a week and just last week they went to see Tyler Perry's play "*Madea Goes To Jail*."

Jade sipped her cider. "Oh, I see. So they're still playing games with each other."

"Whatever is goin' on platonically, ain't 'cause of Jason, you can be sure of that," Miranda said.

"I can't believe she's still stringing that man along…"

"And straight up, trippin'." Both women laughed.

"I'm still upset with her," Jade admitted.

"Yeah, I know. As a matter of fact I thought you wasn't comin' 'cause of that. I even mentioned it to Ivy on Wednesday when she told me you wasn't comin'."

"If she wasn't my friend I don't think her calling me a tramp would have upset me in the least."

"Well, I think you need to get over it. You know Sheena love you, girl. She just talks without thinkin' sometimes and you know how she is. She's always voiced her opinion."

"That was one opinion she could have kept to herself." Jade snapped.

"You know, Jade, you really need to just squash it. It happened over two years ago and all the woman said was that you're *acting* like a tramp. The key word here is *acting*."

"No, Randi, she called me a whore."

"I was there and she didn't say that."

"Look, let's just forget it, all right?"

After a short pause Miranda said, more quietly, "Do me a favor, Jade, and don't start nothin' with Sheena when she gets here. Let's enjoy each other's company 'cause Ivy don't need to be around no drama, okay?"

Jade rolled her eyes at Miranda, who was firm. "I mean it, Jade."

"Okay. No drama, I'll be good." Jade conceded, throwing her hands in the air.

"Thank you."

After a few moments Jade looked at Miranda, "It's just a shame that she can't see a good thing at the tip of her nose."

"I got to agree, in my book Jason is considered a good catch. I for one couldn't be so lucky as to get a B-M-W who has an A-P-T and a C-A-R," Miranda giggled.

Jade was now giggling, too. "BMW, we're not talking about a car, right?"

"No, silly, I'm talkin' 'bout a *Black Man Working*."

"And the A-P-T part?"

"Apartment. You know most of these brothers are still at home with their mamas," Miranda clarified.

"Oh, okay. So CAR is simply a man with his own transportation."

"Now you're with me. Bus tokens just put a damper on a date!"

Ivy reentered the room and sat at the table. "What's so funny?"

"The lack of B-M-W who has an A-P-T and a C-A-R," Jade answered lightly, still smiling. Ivy stared at her. Jade waved her hand. "Never mind. Randi can explain it to you later. What's up?"

Ivy ran her fingers through her hair, then exhaled. "That was Cooper Medical Center."

Instantly the air felt charged and the laughter dissipated. "What's up, Ivy?" Jade asked again.

"Ray's at the hospital. They want me to come over there."

"Well, come on, I'll–"

Ivy cut Miranda off. "I'm not going to the hospital to see about him. Let his woman take care of him."

"I can feel you on that," Miranda nodded empathetically. "Now let's have a group hug."

After embracing each other in sisterly love, Ivy was the first to pull away, wiping tears from her eyes. Standing back, she looked at both women who she knew as true friends and, directing her attention to Miranda, "You've really grown up, baby cousin." She smiled at her. Tilting her head, she changed her tone of voice and sternly added, "But don't you ever raise your voice to me again, you cow. I'm still your elder."

They all burst out laughing. It was a much-needed good feeling to be together again.

Chapter Three

For the next hour, Ivy poured her heart out to her friends.

She told them that Ray received a monthly pension from the NFL and that she had not seen a penny of it in almost a year. She put the house up for sale a month ago because she could no longer make the monthly mortgage payment. She had sold the baby grand piano and numerous other items purely for survival.

The family's investments and entire savings had been blown away on Ray's addiction, which included some of the most expensive treatment centers in the country. After that didn't work out, Ivy made the mistake of not cutting back her expenses sooner than she did. Ray's squandering and womanizing had made matters even worse.

Ray had begun taking drugs during the last year of his football career. Initially it was not for recreation, but to relieve the aches and pains he was experiencing from injuries sustained on the playing field. He told Ivy that the painkillers the doctors prescribed had not helped. But a combination of both street and prescription drugs made him comfortable, enabling him to perform on the field.

Miranda and Jade listened to the story, mesmerized.

The phone rang for the second time and Ivy excused herself to answer it. It was the hospital calling, yet again. Now she was agitated, exhausted and disheartened by the retelling of her sorry tale – and she didn't need this on top of it. She had already told them that she was not going there to see about her estranged husband. Once should have been enough.

She looked over at Miranda and Jade, who were sitting at the kitchen table, using a calculator to go over her household bills, and murmured to them, "It's the hospital again." She paused for a moment, listening to what the man on the other end of the phone had to say. After a short pause, she said, "Okay, okay, I'll be there."

She slammed the phone down onto its hook. "That is, when hell freezes over!"

Miranda frowned. "Somethin' has got to be seriously wrong for them to call here twice, Ivy. Come on, let's go." Miranda stood up, ready for action.

"I'm not stepping a foot in that hospital. Forget him. I'm not going anywhere," Ivy snapped.

"Look, Ivy, the man could be critically wounded or something," Jade added another dimension to the possibilities.

Ivy would not budge. She was mad. Going over her bills with her friends, talking about her past for the last hour had made her even more upset with Ray. The pain and humiliation she was going through were because of him. He'd allowed it all to happen. Just thinking about being homeless was enough to make her let him bleed to death.

"Well, that's just too bad," replied Ivy. "If he needs intensive care or critical care, he's in the right place. They even have a shock and trauma unit right there."

Jade and Miranda debated with Ivy for the next fifteen minutes, trying to talk her into going to see about Ray. But Ivy was stubborn, and Ray needing her was just the medicine she needed for her bruised ego. Oh, she could hardly wait to rub this in his face. Just two weeks ago she had told him, *you'll need me before I need you.* She just hadn't thought it would be this soon.

All Ivy's important bills were being settled on Monday, thanks to her friends. Miranda phoned her aunt and uncle and told them about Ivy's circumstances, and they agreed to pay up her mortgage. After Sheena called to let them know she was unable to meet them until the following day they gave her the scope on what they now were calling Ivy's Dilemma. Sheena instructed them to do what they could and she would handle the rest. Ivy felt such warmth and love from her friends, and an incredible sense of relief that was good... even though she knew it was temporary.

And then, as if on cue, the phone rang for the third time. Again, it was the hospital. Miranda answered it this time, and the caller never asked to speak to Ivy. He simply barked into the phone, "Mrs. Miller, this is Cooper Medical Center again. Are you coming to the hospital or not?"

Miranda was put off for a moment. She couldn't believe this was a professional call. "Is this really the hospital?"

"Yes, it is, and it's very important that you get here as quickly as humanly possible."

"Why?"

There was a pause. "It's better that you come in person, Mrs. Miller." The voice was gentler now. "It really is."

"Thank you. I'm on my way." Miranda hung up the phone.

"You're on your way where?" Ivy asked, mystified.

"No, girlfriend, *we* are on our way to Cooper Hospital."

"When hell freezes over," Ivy repeated her earlier mantra.

"Well, consider it frozen!" Miranda started toward her.

"I'm not going anywhere!" Ivy ranted at Miranda, who shook her head. Ivy sat with her arms folded across her breast and her lips pouting. "I'm not going," she said with finality.

The phone rang again; this time it was Ray's sister Lisa. Ivy refused to take the call. "What do you want me to say, Ivy?" Ivy rolled her eyes at Miranda, not answering her question.

"Let me speak to her," Jade took the phone from Miranda.

"Hi, Lisa, this is Jade. Ivy can't take your call at the moment. Just give me the message and I'll be sure that she gets it."

Ivy and Miranda watched as Jade listened to the message, saying "okay" a few times and then finally saying, "Me and Randi will bring her. See you in a few." She hung up the phone, "Look, Ivy, Lisa said that she's at the hospital with your brother and they won't give them any information. They'll only talk to you. They need you down there. Now."

Ivy hesitated. "Well, if I'm going down there, then at least let me put some decent clothes on," she said, pouting. "I'm going to make my face up too. I'll be damned if I let him and his woman see me looking bad."

The phone rang again. This time it was Ivy's brother-in-law, Peter, wanting to know if she was coming to the hospital. Miranda told him they were on their way.

* * *

They arrived at the hospital an hour later. Ivy's brother, John, was already there with Ray's youngest sister, Lisa. They were standing outside the emergency entrance. Ivy felt some surprise seeing him, then she remembered that John and Lisa had been dating for several months.

"They won't tell us anything," John said to his sister as she joined the group.

"I called Mama, and she's on her way," Lisa added her bit of information.

A nurse met them at the entrance and they were ushered immediately into a room off to the side of the lobby area.

"Who's Mrs. Miller?" the nurse asked.

"I am," Ivy answered.

"Only one of you can come back with her," the nurse informed them.

"Randi," Ivy said, reaching for her cousin. *What in the world has happened to Ray,* she thought.

They were escorted to a small room off the treatment area where they sat down, and almost immediately were joined by two men. "Mrs. Miller, I'm Dr. Grant, and this is Officer Brown," he greeted as he reached out for a handshake. "Please don't stand," he added as he reached for a chair opposite them.

Miranda knew immediately there was something dreadfully wrong. She grasped her cousin's hand.

"What? Just tell me what it is," Ivy couldn't keep the alarm out of her voice.

"Your husband was brought here after a car accident he was involved in on Route 70 in Cherry Hill," the policeman explained. "His car was traveling on the wrong side of the road, and he was hit head-on by a truck."

Dr. Grant added, "Mrs. Miller, he was in serious condition when he arrived. He wasn't breathing on his own..."

At that moment, Ivy's ears seemed to shut down. All she could see was the man's mouth moving and nothing coming out. Then she heard him say, "We did all we could. However, his internal injuries were just too extensive. We lost him at 6:20."

"What? What do you mean you lost him? Lost who?"

The two men looked at each other. "Your husband, Mrs. Miller," said Dr. Grant gently. "We lost your husband. His neck was broken in the accident. We did all we could,"

"Lost him? You mean Ray's dead?" she asked in total disbelief. "He's dead?

The doctor nodded, understanding her shock. "Yes; he was brought here around a quarter to six tonight. We worked very hard to save him. There was just too much internal bleeding and we couldn't stop it."

Ivy pulled her hand free from Miranda's, stood up, and walked toward the window. She stared out, unseeing.

"Ivy?" Miranda's voice was concerned.

"I want to know one thing. Who was in the car with him?" She did not move from her position at the window.

"Pardon me?" both men asked in unison, startled.

She spun around quickly and looked the policeman directly in his eyes, her voice becoming strident. "Who was in the car with him? I know he wasn't alone."

Officer Brown looked at his notes and answered, "Her name is Caroline Hall."

"I don't believe this." She spoke out loud, words that were meant for herself. "Is she dead, too?"

"No, ma'am, she was only shaken up. She hardly has a scratch on her," the officer answered.

"Well, isn't that just grand?" Ivy asked sarcastically. "That's all I needed to know, gentlemen." She nodded to them in salutation. "Let's go, Randi."

The doctor made a movement of protest. "Mrs. Miller, you have to identify the body, and we must release your husband's belongings to you."

"Give them to Caroline Hall. Randi, let's go."

"We can't do that."

"Why? You said she's not dead." Ivy began to laugh and both men looked at her in horror, despite understanding the many variations that shock can take. "Isn't that something? She's in the same accident that killed my husband, but the witch still lived. Well, she had him in life, she can have him in death, too."

"Mrs. Miller, we can only release his things to you," the doctor said.

"Take the stuff, Ivy. I'll come with you to identify him," Miranda assured her.

Ivy immediately stopped laughing. "No, I'm out of here." She was livid. She turned and bolted out of the room.

Family members had begun to arrive and gather in the lobby of the emergency area. Ray's brother Peter was the first one Ivy noticed, then Lisa, John, and a few of Ray's friends. They all asked the same questions.

"What's going on, Ivy?" "What's wrong with him?" "Is he okay?"

Jade stood and walked over to Ivy and Miranda. Miranda whispered to Jade for a moment. Jade gasped and covered her mouth after hearing that Ray was dead.

"What's going on?" Ivy heard the words but didn't respond. She didn't even know who had asked them. "Jade, please take me home." She started to walk toward the exit.

"What did they say, Ivy?" Lisa asked. Ivy felt badgered.

"Why could they only speak to you?" Ray's brother Peter asked.

Could she repeat the same garbage the doctor just told her about Ray? No, it couldn't be true. Did the man really say he was dead?

Feeling pressured to answer, Ivy turned to the crowd and announced, "They said his neck is broken."

There was a collective gasp. "Can we see him?" Peter asked.

"I didn't even see him," she blurted out.

"Why wouldn't they let you see him? Lisa asked.

John had a thought of his own. "Well, if you didn't see him, how do you know it's him? It could be someone else."

"That's right. Someone could have stolen his wallet and have his I.D." Lisa was clearly grasping at straws in her panic.

"Ivy, you really do need to be sure it's him," Miranda pleaded. "Right now you're the only one who can put the speculation to rest."

"Who else would be with Caroline?" Ivy asked rhetorically. She stopped to think for a moment and finally threw up her hands, "Okay, Okay, I'll go back in there. Come on, Randi," she commanded.

They went back in and Miranda told the nurse that they wanted to see Ray. They were led to the room where he lay.

Ivy knew as soon as she saw the top of his head that it was indeed him. She went to the left side of the gurney and looked down into his face and noticed that his eyes were slightly opened. She was fuming. *If he would have had his behind at home where he belonged, he wouldn't be here lifeless,* she thought.

Out loud, she said, "Ain't this some mess, Randi? He's leaving me here to raise these kids by myself. If he weren't already dead, I'd kill him myself. Damn you, Ray," she said. "Damn you, damn you!"

Miranda realized how sad the whole situation was. This was the same man Ivy loved and had married, standing before God and their entire family, only eleven years ago! Now she was acting as if she didn't care a thing about him. Miranda knew she had to be stressed – that she was probably in shock. This was so unlike Ivy, who was generally warm, impulsive, caring. The Ivy she knew would be weeping over her husband's body. The Ivy she knew would have been reaching out to his family, no matter how hurt she had been by them. The Ivy she knew wasn't vindictive, cold, or unfeeling.

And yet this Ivy suddenly seemed to be all of those things.

Ivy walked to the other side of the gurney. She looked closer at Ray. Then looked at Miranda and said, bitterly, "Let's go."

Miranda followed her out, allowing her cousin space to feel whatever it was she needed to feel.

"Mrs. Miller, these are your husband's personal things," the nurse called to her.

Miranda paused as Ivy continued to walk as if she didn't hear a thing the woman had said. "I'll take them," Miranda responded. "As you can see, my cousin is very upset."

Simply saying that she was upset was too mild an explanation for her cousin's attitude toward her deceased husband, but Miranda didn't know what else she could say. Ivy was infuriated and she didn't care who knew it. She didn't realize how much of her anger was due to grief: the anger was easier to feel.

When they got back to the waiting area, Ivy saw that her in-laws had arrived. As soon as they saw her, the barrage of questions came at her again. "Did you see him, Ivy? Is it him?"

"Yes, I saw him, and he's dead," she said coldly, without an ounce of compassion in her voice.

Lisa slumped back in her chair and howled. "No, no, no!"

"Lord, Jesus, Lord, Jesus, my baby, not my baby boy," his mother shouted in anguish.

Ivy looked at them all one by one consoling each other. Who was there for her? Not even her brother, who was holding Ray's sister in his arms as she wept. No, nobody was there for her. That made her even more furious. Ray had been walking all over her for almost two years. Yet not one person had compassion for her. *Well, forget them all,* she thought. She was glad Ray was dead. Now she could get out of this whole nightmare and find her a real man who would appreciate her.

Jade stood next to Ivy and stroked her back.

Miranda stood on the other side of her. "What cha wanna do?"

One lonely tear trickled down Ivy's face, "Come on, Randi, Jade. I have to go and tell my babies that their daddy won't ever be coming home again."

They walked out of the hospital just as the news crew was arriving.

Chapter Four

Ivy paced the floor of her parent's bedroom after hanging up the phone. Ray's mother had been on the line. If Ivy had been angry before, she was downright furious now. "I'd slide his behind in a paper bag and plant him in his mother's backyard if I could," she spat out in anger, stopping her pacing.

Her parents watched in shock. They had never seen their daughter act this way; but they had also never seen her under this much stress. Her father understood a little of what was going on; as a pastor, he had often been near people who were in shock, and it can manifest itself in many different ways.

On the other hand, much of Ivy's anger was well-placed. Her mother-in-law was clearly making the experience of Ivy's husband's death worse than it had to be. In this situation, they felt, both families should be coming together with an abundance of love and support for one another. Instead, this whole ordeal had been nothing but self-centered drama from the start.

"Ivy, baby, if you don't calm down you're going to blow a gasket," her mother warned.

Ivy didn't seem to hear her. "Do you believe her nerve, Mama? No, I can believe it," she continued, answering her own question.

"Who are you talking about, Anna or Carson?" Ivy's father asked.

"Miss Queen Hell-Raiser herself, Anna B. Miller, my dear mother-in-law, who else?" Ivy answered with sarcasm. "She was always asinine. The moron. What would make now any different?"

Ivy took a deep breath, leaned against her mother's bureau, and thought about a time when Anna didn't have so much hostility toward her. There were good memories, back then. When she was eleven or twelve years old, Anna had taught her how to make rag dolls. Ivy never knew how to sew until Anna taught her several stitching techniques. Ivy still had some of those dolls today; she had saved them for her own children. "I never understood why she just stopped liking me. I never did anything to that woman. I've always respected her, but ever since Ray and I got married, she's turned into a certified witch but with a capital B."

"Actually, she started acting a fool before you and Ray got married," Ivy's mother corrected. "She's the only person that's ever made me so angry that I wanted to temporarily lay down my religion and go ballistic on her."

"Well, it's a good thing you never had to fight that bear. She outweighs you by a hundred pounds," Ivy's father joked.

Anna B. Miller was an Amazon, but extremely regal. Her short mixed silver gray hair was never out of place, her makeup flawless. A retired English teacher, she always spoke with perfect diction. Her husband Carson was shorter than she and the perfect example of opposites attracting. He was a retired railroad worker who had never completed high school, a submissive man who hardly ever spoke.

"That bear would have needed a stick to whoop me," Ivy's mother retorted.

Her husband reached over and took her hand comfortingly. "Ah now, don't get yourself all worked up, honey. She's been upset with you ever since you kicked her out of our house twelve years ago, and even angrier with Ivy for marrying Ray in the first place."

Ivy stopped pacing, folded her arms across her chest, and exhaled in frustration. "You know something, I just don't want to fight her anymore, Daddy. If she wants to handle all the funeral arrangements for her baby boy, then so be it."

"It doesn't make a difference what Anna wants to do," her father said to her. "Ray was your husband, and you can do whatever *you* want to do. You hold the power unless you choose to relinquish it. You need to think about what's best for you – and for your children. They're the ones that count here."

"That's right, honey," her mother said in agreement. "All you need to do is call the funeral home and tell them to pick up his body. The arrangements…"

"What are you talking about, Mama?" Ivy asked. "I don't care. Ray's mother can have everything her way. And she can pay for the funeral too. I'm not doing a thing." Ivy sighed, feeling the weight of her husband's betrayal even heavier than that of his death. "She said that Ray left everything to her and her husband, and that they would handle all the funeral arrangements. So let them. They have the means to pay for it, 'cause Lord knows I don't. But you know what really makes me mad? It's the fact that even now that he's gone, she won't even give me enough respect to acknowledge that I am his wife, the mother of her son's children. Now you tell me if that's not some mess? Treating me like I don't have a say in what happens at my own husband's funeral." Ivy lifted her hand and pointed it toward the bedroom door. "Those are his babies out there who don't have a father anymore. Did she even ask if the children were okay? No, all she wanted to know was if I had called Johnson's Funeral Home to tell them that she would be handling the arrangements." She placed her hands on her hips. "Mama, you know I wouldn't use Johnson's Funeral Home if they were the last place on earth to send my husband's body to."

Ivy broke off and walked over to the window, then turned to face her mother. "Why can't she be a grandmother to my babies, Mama? Why can't she show them a little affection? Even if I *had* filed for divorce, according to the law, I'm still his wife. Look how he left us, deprived and destitute." Her voice rose as she spoke.

"Well, even if he did leave them everything, I'm sure as his wife you have rights to–"

"He had nothing to leave anyone," Ivy interrupted.

"What do you mean, he had nothing? I'm sure you can bury him with the money from his life insurance policy," her mother replied, trying to sound as comforting as she could.

"Insurance? What insurance?"

"Ivy, you had to have had insurance on Ray," her father said, standing up with sudden energy, pacing, turning to lean against the closet door. For the first time, he looked worried.

"Daddy, you're not getting it. I could barely keep food on the table. How in the world was I going to continue to pay on an insurance policy on that no-count Negro?" That got a reaction; Her father raised his bald head, straightened up, looking at her sternly. She paused and took a deep breath in an effort to calm herself. She knew she had just spoken in a disrespectful manner to her father. "I'm sorry, Daddy," she said apologetically. "I didn't mean to raise my voice to you." Her father relaxed and nodded, accepting the apology. She focused on the tone of her voice and said, "I don't have the money to bury him, so just let them do whatever they want to do," she said again with a wave of her hand.

She began to pace again.

Ivy's mother walked over to her and stopped her pacing by hugging her tightly. Like any mother in a similar situation, had she been able to, she would have taken on all the pain and suffering her child was facing. And again like all mothers, the most she could do was to give her child the moral support needed to endure this trying time. "You have us, sweetie, and we're better than money in your pocket."

Ivy's father came to stand with them in the middle of the floor. "This family has always stuck together during bad times, so don't you worry about the money. You do what you want, and we'll take care of the bill." Ivy broke down and cried, holding on to her parents.

Her mother walked her over to the bed. "Come on, sit down, honey. Try and relax a little now."

Ivy was perplexed. For months she had tried to figure out where she had gone wrong, if there had been anything she could have done to save her husband from self-destruction. Even after Ray stopped attending weekly church services, she continued to keep his name before the altar in prayer. She had been taught long ago, through her grandfather's ministry, that the husband is sanctified by the wife, and the wife by the husband. So why had God forsaken her? She had been devoted to the church and to her family, even though her husband had turned his back on God and the family. She wanted answers and she wanted them now. So she asked the question she thought her parents might be able to answer for her.

"Why is this happening to me, Mama? I've tried all my life to live right by doing what is required of me as a Christian wife. I've never been with anyone but my husband. And I never even let him touch me until we were married. Why is God punishing me? I don't understand." Ivy was a PK, a Preacher's Kid. The family came from a long line of preacher's kids. Her mother's father was a PK, her father's father had been her pastor from the time she was born until his death the year after she and Ray married. The pastorate had been passed to his son, Ivy's father. Ivy's husband, Ray, had been licensed as a missionary minister when he was only twenty-one years old. His college football team nicknamed him the minister of defense.

So with this background, it was clear that Ivy had always tried to stay in the will of God. Even as a teenager, when her peers tried to entice her, she didn't behave in any way other than as a Christian. Ivy had always stood her ground and stayed rooted to her moral upbringing.

Now she wondered why.

"God is not punishing you," her mother said gently. "Ray made the mistake of leaving his spiritual family, as well as you and the children. Now, I'm sorry to say it, but it's too late for Ray. If he wasn't right with God before he closed his eyes then it's too bad, so sad. You keep your hands in God's hand, girl. Ray may have left you, but God will never leave you or forsake you. Don't you worry, baby. Weeping may endure for a night, but joy comes in the morning."

Her father put his hand under her chin, turned her face toward him, and picked up where his wife had left off. "Baby, God won't put more on you than you can bear. I've always taught you that it rains on the just, as well as the unjust. Just remember that it's only after the rain that the beauty of a rainbow can be seen, and withered flowers are able to blossom to their fullest potential. You're a flower, baby. You've been withering in the sun too long without the rain. Now when the rain stops falling, you're going to be stronger than ever because I know God's got a plan."

A knock on the bedroom door interrupted her father's impromptu sermon. Miranda peeked her head through the doorway, gesturing to Ivy that she had another telephone call. Ivy rolled her eyes to the ceiling and thought, *what now*? Picking up the telephone extension in the bedroom she answered the call.

Ivy was still on the phone when Miranda appeared at the door again. This time it was to announce that Ray's sister, Lisa, was here to see her.

Ivy's mother responded. "Tell Lisa she'll be out in a minute."

Miranda wasn't so sure it was a good idea. "You sure, Aunt Pat?"

Her aunt confirmed with a nod of her head.

"Absolutely not," Ivy was saying to the caller. "No! I don't give a rat's hairy behind. No one will be going in my house or through my things!" She paused, then said, "Do whatever you have to do. It's my house until the damn sheriff's department padlocks it for the mortgage company. And, until that time, I say who will and will not enter 4321 Pleasant Drive." She slammed the phone down. "They have lost their ever-loving minds," she said to her parents.

"Who was it this time?" her father asked.

"That was Ray's brother, Peter. He wants to come into my house and get some things that belong to Ray." She paused and began pacing the floor again. "Is it me, or what? Are they crazy? Whatever was Ray's belongs to his children now. What is wrong with those people?"

"What is it they want of Ray's?" her mother asked with surprise.

"It doesn't matter what they want," Ivy said through clenched teeth. "I'm not letting them in my house. I'm not giving them anything unless Ray had a will saying that I have to, or until the lawyer tells me to give it up. Every one of them are jackasses. And I do mean all of them."

"Ivy, that's not a nice thing to say. You need to calm down," her father said, watching her pace the floor in a tizzy.

"I'm trying, Daddy. I'm really, really trying. I'm just so angry I don't know what to do." The pacing continued.

"I know, baby, and you have every right to be upset, but you have to calm down. You can't be thinking rationally when you're as angry as you are." He was worried, too. Where were the tears? Where was the grief? Ivy's anger would carry her through only so far.

Ivy continued to pace the floor until she heard another knock on the door. It was Miranda, again, letting her know Ray's sister was still waiting to speak to her.

"Ooh, what does she want?" Ivy asked impatiently. Having just hung up with her brother-in-law, Ivy was not sure she wanted to see her sister-in-law.

"She didn't say," Miranda answered. "Should I tell her you're indisposed?"

"Just bring her in here with us, Miranda," Ivy's mother said.

"Please, Mom," Ivy pleaded. "I don't want to talk to any of them. Don't make me. I can't take any more."

"Let's find out what she wants. Let her in, Randi."

As soon as Lisa entered the bedroom, she could feel the tension around her. She knew the situation between her parents and her brother's wife all too well. Long before Lisa was old enough to make her own conclusions about Ivy, her parents had influenced her thinking. However, as she got older, she began to form her own opinion and she had come to realize that her parents' dislike for Ivy was totally unfounded. And like her brother, she had fallen deeply in love with a Jones, Ivy's younger brother. They had begun dating only six months ago, but Lisa had already had a crush on him for most of her life.

To tell the truth, Lisa had never really had a chance to be around Ivy other than those times her brother would come get her to babysit Ray Junior for them, back when she was still in high school. It was during that time Lisa observed the love Ivy had for her brother first-hand. It was also during that time that Lisa was able to discard all the negative rumors about her brother's wife.

Ivy refused to allow her feelings to be subjected to Anna Miller's wrath after the first year of her marriage. Ivy had spent her first married Christmas alone, crying, after her mother-in-law had pretended to have a heart attack. Not knowing at the time how vicious and conniving his mother could be, Ray had rushed to her side, leaving Ivy at home alone.

Ivy had tried to tell Ray that if in fact it had been real, the hospital would have never released her a mere two hours after being rushed in by ambulance; but he ignored her and gave in to his mother's theatrics.

Right now Lisa was nervous. She was nervous because she knew first-hand that her mother had always been unfair to Ivy. She knew that Ivy had her guard up anytime she had to interact with any members of the Miller family. *What was the proper way to approach her?* Lisa thought. Ivy's brother John advised her to merely be herself. He felt that doing so would allow Ivy to see her for the loving person she is.

"I just want you to know I'm here for you." Lisa looked down at the floor as she spoke, trying to find the right words to say. "I know my mother can really be a pain, and I'm truly sorry about that. I just want to be here for you, as well as my nieces and nephews. I just wanted you to know that."

Lisa raised her head then, looking directly at Ivy for the first time. Ivy took a deep breath. *She isn't like the rest of them at all.* Actually, Lisa reminded her of herself. She wanted to do right. Tears seeped from Ivy's eye. "I appreciate that, Lisa. Actually, you can help me a whole lot. My kids could use your support right now. I'm no good to them at the moment."

Lisa brightened at the opportunity to mend fences, to help Ivy out. "I'd be happy to," she responded enthusiastically. "If it's all right with you, I'll take them to my apartment for a while. We can hang out together, and I'll take good care of them, help them to talk about feeling sad if you want. You can call me when you're ready for them to come home."

"Thank you, Lisa. That will help me a lot."

Lisa smiled sadly as she came closer to Ivy with outstretched arms and squeezed her sister-in-law in a hug.

Ivy broke down in tears.

Chapter Five

Jason Jackson knew immediately, just from the way that Sheena answered her cell phone, that something dreadful had happened. He listened to her words with a growing sense of dread. "Oh, my God! Randi, I'm so sorry to hear that. Tell Ivy I'm so sorry and that I'll be there as soon as humanly possible." She looked at her watch. "Jason and I had a case in North Carolina and we're on our way home now."

The timing could hardly be worse from Jason's point of view. Something spectacularly awful had apparently happened, claiming Sheena's attention, just when he had finally worked up his courage to tell her about his feelings for her.

Only seconds before the phone rang, he had been saying, "From the first time I laid eyes on you I knew you were special. I'm in love with you, Sheena, and I can't help myself."

And, of course, just as he was telling her what was in his heart and on his mind, her cell phone rang. Worse still, she interrupted what he was saying to answer it.

He sat instead and thought about their shared past. Jason and Sheena had met when she was a law clerk in Bill Hart's office. Jason had had an appointment with Bill to discuss a case he was assigned when the most exquisite woman he had ever seen walked through the doors of the conference room with Bill following behind her. Jason's mouth dropped as his eyes followed her as she seemingly floated, with the grace of a swan, into the room. Her skin was flawless. She stretched out her hand toward him looking directly in his eyes. "Hi, I'm Sheena Daniels." Her light brown eyes sparkled like diamonds. The woman had him in a trance. He realized he was staring at her when he heard Bill ask if he was all right.

Regaining his composure, Jason apologized for staring at her. Finally he touched her outstretched hand for a shake and that touch was far more potent than his attraction to her physical appearance. Or maybe it was the combination of both that knocked him off his feet.

Jason did not see Sheena after that day until five months later when she came to work for the US Department of Education in the Philadelphia office. She was assigned to his division. Jason could hardly believe his luck. But after three years he was still unable to penetrate the iron-clad fortress she had built around herself. He wanted her the day he met her and he still wanted her now.

Jason needed her to know what was in the depths of his heart. He could tell that at first she didn't know what to say after she heard him say, *I'm in love with*

you. His frankness had caught her totally off-guard, but he could see the moment his words sank in. The expression on her face illuminated his understanding.

She turned in her seat and raised her head, looking at him sternly, "We agreed a long time ago to be friends. Why have you changed your mind?"

And then her cell phone rang.

"How did it happen?" she asked into the phone. She touched Jason on the arm and mouthed to him, "Ray Miller was killed yesterday in a car accident."

As soon as she gave him that news, he knew that their discussion was over, at least for the time being.

* * *

Saturday afternoon, Jade and Miranda watched in horror from the living room window as Ray's brother Peter pulled into the driveway of Ivy's home – with Caroline Hall in the car with him.

Peter was six inches shorter than his brother and much more attractive. But his personality was never as friendly at Ray's. Everyone that knew him had the impression that he was jealous of his brother.

"Lock the screen door, Randi. Don't let them in the house!"

Miranda rushed to the door to ensure it was locked. Jade watched from the bay window as Peter strolled up the brick herringbone walkway.

"Get the phone, get the phone!" Miranda ordered. Jade retrieved the cordless phone and then stood near Miranda at the front door.

"Well, the poop is about to hit the fan now," Jade said for Miranda's ears only.

As Peter approached the front door, he greeted Miranda, standing guard like a British soldier at the queen's residence. "Hey, Randi." He looked past her and greeted Jade simply by her name, "Jade." When neither woman answered, he asked, "Can I speak to Ivy?" trying, as he did, to open the screen door.

"I'm not letting you in, Peter," Miranda said point-blank.

"Look, I just need to talk to Ivy. I need some things of Ray's to take to the funeral home."

Miranda continued to hold him with her gaze. "You are low, Peter. You come here to my grieving cousin's home with her deceased husband's lover and then have the audacity to pull into her driveway – wanting what, Peter? To hurt her more than she already is?" She shook her head in total disgust. "Well, I don't think so. You really have balls the size of an elephant."

"What happened between my brother and his wife had nothing to do with me," Peter objected. "I was a friend of Caroline's long before they started seeing each other. As a matter of fact, Miss Thing, Ray took her from *me*, just like he did with most of the women in my life, from the time we were teenagers. And this includes your dear cousin, my sister-in-law."

Miranda stepped closer to the screen door, almost touching her face to it. "You are pathetic, a real piece of human slime. Ivy never wanted you and you know it. She's always been in love with Ray from the moment she saw him the day your family moved in next door to her. You know that, and I know that. Ivy doesn't deserve the total disrespect and disregard of feelings your whole family has displayed." She lowered her voice still more, so that it came out as a hiss. "But you know what, Peter? You're going to pay. Your mother is going to pay, your father is going to pay, and do you know why? Because God don't like ugly and right now all three of you look like monsters straight from hell."

"Is that right?" he answered sarcastically.

Miranda responded with attitude. "Oh, did I stutter? Yeah, that's right. You reap what you sow, my brother, the good and the bad. Now, I don't know what your family's beef is and I really don't give a fart in space. But if you all thought that the Jones family was going to idly stand by and let your family roll all over Ivy in her weakened state, then you all thought wrong. My uncle may be turning the other cheek, but all of us ain't that saved yet. I swear, as God is my witness, I'll pop a cap in your behind. Now get out of my face and take that trash in the car with you. And don't come back here again unless you come correct. Ivy's family is taking care of the funeral and all the details."

He was livid. "You don't know who…"

Without moving her gaze from him, Miranda said, "Jade, I think it's time to dial 9-1-1."

"This ain't over, Randi." Peter was blustering now, trying to save face.

"No, I'm sure it isn't. But in the meantime, my family will certainly be contacting your family to let you all know what arrangements have been made for your brother's funeral. Jade?"

"Nine," Jade confirmed, then paused, holding the telephone ostentatiously in her hand.

Everyone looked toward the car that had just pulled into the driveway next to Peter's. Miranda murmured, "It's Sheena."

"One," Jade said and paused again. Jason and Sheena got out of the car. Sheena glanced at Caroline and nearly did a double-take as she walked past the car.

Jade spoke again. "Do I really need to dial the last digit, Peter?"

He turned and walked away.

Chapter Six

Night fell, and finally, the house was quiet.

It was too quiet for Jade. The silence gave her the opportunity to think about the things she had come to Ivy's house to ignore, however temporarily. What could she have done to avoid being in the dilemma in which she found herself? That was a question she had asked herself during her three-hour drive to Ivy's house.

She should have told Darrell about her pregnancy from the very beginning. No – maybe she should have told him after she had already had the child. No – there would never be a good time to tell him, not unless her plans were to be with him for the rest of her life. She knew that was what he wanted.

From the first day they met, he'd talked about how important family was to him, about how one day he wanted to marry and have children. So she knew he felt strongly about the whole institution of marriage. His mother and father had been married for over thirty years. Darrell wanted to get married and step into the ministry to which he believed God had called him.

But there was no way she could live up to the expectations put upon a minister's wife. Jade knew there were still some things Darrell didn't know about her. She knew in her heart of hearts that when he found out the real truth, he would move on and find himself a woman more deserving of his love.

That's why she had left early on a Friday morning with all intentions of keeping her son away from his father. She called her boss and told him that she had a family emergency and needed to take a leave of absence, knowing that she would probably never come back. She had to disappear, just leave the country and everything behind and start a new life where no one knew her. Then she realized how silly that was. What about her family? What about her twelve-year-old sister whom she loved dearly? There was no way she could easily drop out of sight and leave her. How could she?

She glanced at the clock on the wall. *Almost three o'clock in the morning*, she muttered. She had glanced at the clock less than five minutes ago. There was no sleeping for her tonight. Her mind kept wandering to what had happened last Thursday.

What had happened was that Darrell had found her.

He had hired a private investigator to track her down. He even had the baby's birth certificate. She knew the document held no information on it because, when filling out the vital static application, she had written, "father unknown."

It was her child's facial resemblance to him that had given her away.

Two weeks before he found her, she had gone out with a friend and her two children to see the Soul Circus. It never occurred to her that someone from Philadelphia would be in Greenville, South Carolina, attending the event. Yet there, standing in front of her at the concession stood, Michael Williams – who just happened to be one of Darrell's closest friends. Her baby was on her hip and there was no way to avoid him seeing her son. Michael never asked who the baby was, but Jade knew from the way he stared at her that he didn't have to ask.

"Hey, girl, you got your arms full, so I guess a hug is out of the question," Michael had said to Jade, recovering quickly.

"This is true," she answered. "How are you, Michael?"

"I'm well." He paused. "So this is where you live now?"

"No," she answered before thinking." I drove down with a friend. Her family lives here in Greenville. Look, I need to get back. It was good to see you." She began to walk away.

"Jade!" Michael called after her. She didn't say a word, just looked back at him. "He doesn't know, does he?"

"No, but I know you're about to change that," she answered and walked away.

Jade's thoughts were interrupted as Ivy walked into the room, looking tousled and sleepy. "Hey, Jade. What are you doing still up?"

"I couldn't sleep. The question is, what are *you* doing up?"

"I've been out, for what, eight or nine hours? What did you all give me?"

"Your father told us to give it to you. He's the one who called Dr. Schulman and told him to prescribe something."

"Well, whatever it was, it worked. I'm feeling pretty rested," Ivy said, yawning.

"Good. But it's still the middle of the night." Jade went and sat down next to Ivy, feeling inexplicably protective of her.

"Well, that only means I'm refreshed and ready to hear why you can't sleep. Besides, I know something is troubling you."

Jade shrugged. "What gave you that idea?"

"Cause you've been twisting that ring on your finger since you been here."

Jade looked down to see that she was doing it again. She stopped and ran her hand through her curls. "Yeah, well, there's a lot going on." The admission sounded more exhausted than grudging. "But it's not about me right now. It's about you. This may be a good time to tell you what happened while you were sleeping." Jade told Ivy about Peter coming to the house, and repeated everything Miranda had said to him.

"Well, I guess I'll have to make all the funeral arrangements myself," Ivy conceded.

"Yeah, at this point I think that's best," Jade agreed.

"So Sheena's here?" Ivy asked.

"Yeah, she's asleep in the twins' room."

Ivy glanced over at Jade and watched as her friend looked out into space, twisting her ring again. Ivy blew out a sigh and got Jade's attention. "Now, tell me, what's going on with you."

"No need to talk about me right now.'

"I said spit it out, Jade, right now." Ivy touched her friend's shoulder encouragingly.

Jade paused a moment and looked down at the floor, gathering her thoughts. When she looked back up, she had tears in her eyes. "He's going to try and take him from me, Ivy."

"What? Who? Darrell?

Jade nodded miserably. "He knows. He came to my house Thursday. That's why I tried to call you Friday morning to let you know I changed my mind and was coming here. When I couldn't get you, I called your mother and told her to let you know I was on my way. I just had to get away."

"I'm lost, Jade. You need to start at the beginning."

"Okay." She took a deep breath. "The first thing he said to me, standing in my living room, was, *'Why didn't you tell me, Jade?'* He was choked up, that was obvious. All he kept saying was, *'Why didn't you tell me I had a son?'*

Her first thought had been to deny it, but a blind man could see that Desmond belonged to Darrell. He was a miniature version of his father.

Now she replayed the scene to Ivy, remembering every word as if it were being spoken, once again, in the quiet of Ivy's house.

"How many times did I ask you about the baby, Jade? You lied to me when you said you had lost it. Why did you do that?" When she didn't answer, he asked again, his voice louder, "How could you lie to me, Jade?"

"Please forgive me, Darrell," she said quickly, numbly. After a period of silence and him just staring her down, she murmured, "I'm sorry."

"You're sorry?" he asked, the surprise making his voice sharp. "I don't believe you did this." He knelt down to his son who was sitting on the sofa watching the exchange. "Hey, little man. I'm your daddy," he said to the boy. He tried to pick him up from the sofa, but Desmond moved toward Jade and stretched out his arms for her. Darrell felt humiliated as the boy looked at him.

Jade didn't want a confrontation that could hurt her son. "Please, Darrell. Don't confuse him. He doesn't know you. Let me..."

"I'm his daddy. I'm – Daddy," he said, pointing to his chest, cutting off Jade's plea.

In that moment, Jade realized just how damaging her decision had been. She stood silent, knowing that a grown man – a man she cared about – was about to cry, and she was immediately filled with remorse.

Dee was totally confused by the whole drama. He stared back at his father, then scrambled for Jade to pick him up. She could see Darrell trying his best to keep his composure as he stood up again. He was about to say something else when Jade caught his eye, pleading silently, nodding toward Desmond. This time he considered the child and immediately closed his mouth. She was being protective and she had a right to be. What he wanted to say could not be said in the presence of a child.

"We'll talk after I put him to bed," Jade said. Darrell didn't utter another bitter word.

For the next few hours, they talked quietly, mostly about their son who Jade called Dee. The nickname Dee fit his son; he himself had been called that as a child.

Darrell felt cheated. He had missed the first year and a half of his son's life. He wanted to know everything about him, from birth to the present. So he asked Jade all he could think of, everything that he thought was important to know. Around nine-thirty, Jade allowed Darrell to help her with Dee's bath and getting him ready for bed. Dee was worn out. Darrell sat on the side of Dee's bed while he fell asleep. Darrell took the copy of Dee's birth certificate out of his pocket. He read the child's name from the document. *Desmond Gerald Sanders*. He tightened his month as his eyes gazed at the words, *Father Unknown*.

After a while, Jade came and stood in the doorway and saw how Darrell was looking at her son. It was as if he was trying to remember every feature of his face. She remembered doing that herself when Dee was first born. Feeling Jade's presence, Darrell stood up and walked toward her. Jade stepped back into the hallway as he closed Dee's door. He kept coming toward her, backing her into the banister where he stood staring into her eyes. She didn't like the look on his face. She slid to the side of him and walked down the hall to her bedroom.

He followed her.

After he stepped into the room, he closed the door. Then Darrell began to pace the room. She noticed a sheet of paper in his hand and knew it was the copy of their son's birth certificate. He was fuming.

"Maybe we should talk after you've calmed down." He stopped pacing the floor but was still silent. "Darrell, I didn't mean to keep him away from you. I just..."

Darrell suddenly turned, stood directly in front of her, and tried to say something, but the words just would not form. He made a move as if turning to walk away. Then he abruptly spun around, hitting her with the back of his hand with such force that she fell onto the bed. He leapt on top of her, straddling her. He raised his fist and she immediately cried out, "Oh, Jesus!"

"You —" he cried as he pounded his fist into the pillow right next to her head. "Why, Jade, why?" He wept openly.

She wrapped her arms around him and cried too, and it wasn't because of the stinging on her face. She felt he had a right to be angry. They lay there just like that for a while, crying and holding each other. Finally, he moved away from her. He began to pace the room again in an effort to get his emotions under control. She moved and positioned herself on the side of the bed. He was breathing heavily and she sniffed, trying to dry her tears.

She was startled by his quick turn to her, his return from closeness to anger. He pointed his finger in her face and said, "I want to know why I deserved this, when I know I was good to you. I loved you even after you left me without an explanation. I want the truth about everything right now."

"I think you should sit down."

"I don't want to sit down!" he shouted. "So don't tell me what to do! I need to stand!"

Jade took a deep breath. "I don't have any excuse for what I did. I mean I do, but I don't want to talk about it right now," she quickly amended. "I'll tell you, Darrell – I really will. I just can't right now. There's a reason, and I can't tell you what it is. You have to accept that."

Darrell walked directly in front of her. "Fine, I'm not going to push you." He sat on the bed next to her. "I don't know you at all, do I?"

Jade didn't even attempt to answer.

The pain could be felt from Darrell's voice, "You... you could have told me."

"Look, Darrell, I know I've hurt my son, and you, and myself. I know I was wrong, but I have my reasons."

"But you won't share those reasons with me?"

"Not now. I need to think," Jade pleaded.'

Darrell shook his head. "What do your girls think about your reasons?"

"I haven't told them anything!"

"Come on, Jade. Sheena and Miranda and Ivy are your best friends; they're your girls. You share everything with them. I know they know, and you can't tell me that they don't know."

She slowly shook her head. "They know I had a baby, but they never knew who the father was. I never told them. I only told them that my pregnancy was the reason why I had to leave. So they assumed that the child wasn't yours. And I let them assume just that." Her eyes told him she was being truthful, anyway why would she have to lie now. "They haven't seen me since I had him." She began twisting her ring. "They only saw him as a newborn and at the time, he didn't look like anybody we knew."

Darrell held up the copy of his son's birth certificate. "You should have told me," he was getting angry all over again. He stood and walked over to the bedroom door. "You do know his birth record has to be corrected right?"

"I think there's more important things to worry about..."

"My name isn't on my son's birth certificate." Darrell shook the paper at her. "That's important to me, Jade. He's a Parker not a Sanders and I want his birth record corrected immediately."

Jade turned her head and looked out the window.

"Ooh should I take that gesture as being defiant?"

Still feeling the sting on her face Jade touched her cheek, lifted her head higher and continued to look out the window.

He leaned his back against the wall as he watched her raise her hand to her face briefly touching the bruise. "I'm sorry for hitting you. I was wrong."

"No, you weren't," she protested still looking out the window.

"Yes, I was," he said sternly. "I was wrong. There is no reason why I should have raised a hand to you." He paused a second. "Not even for this. I was wrong, and I'm sorry. I always said that if I ever felt I had to put my hands on a woman, that I didn't need her and she definitely don't need me."

Jade didn't have to ask what he meant. She didn't pretend she didn't know where he was going, either. She just never imagined he would take this approach to the situation.

Jade turned to look at Darrell and was ready to tell him all her secrets.

But then he said, "you've had him to yourself since he was born. It's my turn to have him now," he looked at her coldly.

"Darrell, no! We don't have to fight over him."

"I want him, Jade," he said plainly.

"No, Darrell, please don't do it! Whatever visitations you want..." She hesitated, began twisting the ring on her finger, then tried again. "We can work out some type of reasonable schedule."

He continued to stand at the door, looking down at her in total disgust. To Jade's way of thinking, the silence was an indication that Darrell's mind was twisting and plotting out how he was going to strip all parental rights from her. At that moment, all she could think of was fleeing. She was not going to allow Darrell to take her child.

Darrell was following his own train of thought. "I'll be here tomorrow afternoon. I'm going to take him to meet my parents."

"He can't. He has..."

He cut her off. "I said, I'll be here tomorrow afternoon. I know you get off from work at five, so I'll be here at seven to pick up my son. You have him ready," he growled.

Jade knew that disagreeing with him was out of the question. Tears that she had been holding back were now flowing freely. He stood there watching her without an ounce of sympathy. "I'll let myself out."

Jade watched him from her bedroom window as he got into his Explorer and drove away. Then, and only then, did she break down into uncontrollable tears. She hated that it had come to this.

Jade hardly slept that night and when morning came she called her office arranging a leave of absence, loaded her car and headed for New Jersey on Route 95. She had to get to Ivy. Ivy's life always seemed so perfect to her; Ivy always had the right answers. Jade was hoping she might have some for her.

Now Ivy was watching her with sympathy and incredulity as Jade finished her story. "So you just had to take off and run again?" Ivy asked in disbelief.

"I'm not running. I'm just buying myself some time. So I packed enough clothes for Dee and me to stay gone a month. I needed an intelligent person to talk to, but once I got here, I could see that you had troubles enough of your own. I sure don't want to make anything worse by telling you all this."

Ivy dismissed the thought with a wave of her hand. "You really think he wants to take Dee from you?"

"What else could he mean?" She was twisting the ring again.

"Well, Jade, the man has a right to be teed off at you. He's right, you know: you could have told him."

Jade stared at her, and the silence stretched between them. "Are you going to kick a dog while she's down, or are you going to be my friend?"

"I'm gonna kick a dog while she's down, then be her friend. How could you be so simple, Jade?"

"Don't rag her, Ivy," Sheena said from the doorway. "We all do some stupid things sometimes."

Ivy spun around to look at her. "How long have you been standing there?"

"Long enough to hear that he hit her. And he was right. You didn't deserve to be slapped, even though you think you did." Sheena folded her arms and leaned against the door frame.

Jade got up and walked over to Sheena. She didn't see Sheena's intervention as supportive; she was too tired and too caught up in the past, and chose instead to attack. "You want to know what I really think?" Sheena didn't say anything, and Jade continued, "How is it that you have so much wisdom for others and none for yourself?"

"If you have some wise advise to give me, I'm receptive to it," Sheena's voice dripped sarcasm.

"Well, here's what I think. If I were you, I'd stop pretending to be friends with the man I loved to distraction and set a date to marry him."

"See, that's the problem. You aren't me. But standing on the outside looking in, you think you see everything. What you can't see is beneath and embedded in the colors of the picture. And for that reason, I judge no man."

Jade stepped even closer to Sheena. "Well you sure did judge me when you called me a tramp. Or was it a whore? No, that's right, it was both!"

Sheena was silent.

"I'm going to bed. Good morning, ladies," Jade brushed passed Sheena and walked away.

Sheena and Ivy watched as she exited the room.

Sheena turned to look at Ivy. "I can't believe she's still upset with me about that," clearly astonished.

"Have you ever apologized to her?"

Sheena thought about it for a moment. "No, I don't think I have. I just thought it was forgotten about."

"Well, I think it's well overdue, don't you?"

Without answering Ivy, Sheena walked away in search of Jade.

* * *

Jade walked into her assigned bedroom and plummeted to the bed.

She didn't know why she allowed this thing to rage on between her and Sheena. They had been very close before she told her friend she was pregnant. They had started law school together and for a time they were roommates. *Maybe I should just go to her and tell her just how she hurt me*, she thought just as she heard the rap on the door.

"Jade!" Sheena called.

Jade looked at the closed door. "Yes."

"Can I come in?" Sheena asked. Jade didn't answer. "Please, Jade. I only want a few minutes."

Jade got off the bed, unlocked the door, went back to the bed and sat down on the side of it, then said loudly, "It's open."

Sheena came into the room. "Can I sit down next to you?"

Jade patted the mattress. "Sure."

Sheena sat on the bed. "Look, Jade, I don't want to argue. I know that what I said was wrong, and I apologize. We've been friends since we were in our teens, and I want to remain friends.

Jade took a deep breath. "You know, it's not that you don't have a right to express what you feel, especially since we're supposed to be like sisters. What really hurt is that you lost respect for me."

"No, Jade!"

"Yes, Sheena," she said sternly. "When I told you I had to leave because I was pregnant you asked how could I let that happen. You said I'm supposed to be a virtuous woman. I knew then that you didn't respect me anymore. Then to add insult to injury you call me a whore!"

"I'm sorry. What else do you want me to say or do? But you lied to all of us, Jade. You knew it was Darrell's child all the time. But you made all of us believe that you'd been messin' around while you were dating him. Why?"

"Because I knew you wouldn't understand," she snapped.

"Understand what? You've always been secretive, Jade. You never talk about your childhood. As a matter of fact, we don't know a thing about your life before you came to live here."

"Why is it so important that you know? For goodness' sake. You know the person I am now, that's all that should matter!" Jade paused, "Besides, I had no life before I came here."

How many times had Sheena heard Jade say, *I had no life before I came here*. The room was silent and then Sheena pressed, "I don't want you mad at me. I just wanted to apologize and if you can't accept it, then…" Her voice trailed off.

Jade turned to Sheena and hugged her tightly. Sheena hugged her in return and after she murmured a prayer of thanks, she said, "I'm so glad this is over, 'cause I thought I was going to have to hold you down in a headlock and make you forgive me." They smiled at each other.

Jade heard the little chirp of her cell phone that signaled a missed call. "I don't think I have to guess who it is," she said as she reached for it. Sheena watched as she clicked through the menu under *calls missed*. Jade saw an unfamiliar number and knew it was probably Darrell's.

She looked over at Sheena who had stood up to leave. "I'm not letting him take my baby."

"You don't know what he wants. So call him and ask him plainly what his intentions are. And if he wants a fight, I'll give him the fight of his life."

Jade smiled. "You'd help me?"

"In a heartbeat, even with you mad at me." Both women grinned. "I'm tired, and I'm going to bed." Sheena started out of the room. Before she closed the door, she turned to Jade. "Don't assume what his intentions are, ask him. 'Night." She closed the door.

Jade picked up her cell phone. After a short hesitation, she pushed the unfamiliar number into her keypad.

"Hello?" She could recognize Darrell's deep sexy voice anytime.

"I just need to know one thing," Jade stated without identifying herself.

"What's that, Jade?"

"Are you going to try and take my baby from me?"

"No, Jade. I wouldn't hurt him just to hurt you."

As soon as Darrell gave her that first word, *No*, it was like a ton of bricks had been lifted off her shoulders. She closed the cell phone and breathed a prayer of thanks.

Chapter Seven

Darrell arrived at Ivy's house early Sunday morning. He had heard about Ray's accident on the radio.

"I thought Jade had run out on me when I showed up at her house Friday evening and nobody was there," Darrell explained, standing awkwardly in the front hallway. "I was mad as the devil, thinking she did that just to avoid me. It was the next morning when I found out about Ray, and I knew she was with you all."

"Yeah," Ivy confirmed, "she was the first one here." She dared not tell him that Jade had set out way before the accident ever happened.

"She told me you all didn't know that I was Dee's father."

"I just saw him for the first time on Friday since he was born," Ivy said gently, nodding. "I couldn't believe my eyes, Darrell. He looks so much like you."

"I haven't seen him yet," Miranda said.

"Neither have I," Sheena added, "but Ivy told us how shocked she was to see you were the unknown pop."

"Yeah, I bet. Where is Jade, anyway?"

"She's still asleep. She didn't go to bed last night until about four in the morning."

"She called me around that time, and when she hung up on me I started to call her back. But since I knew where she was, I thought I'd just come over here. I need to talk to her. Can I go and wake her up?"

"You aren't going to start something, are you?" Ivy asked.

"Please don't, 'cause we got enough drama goin' on already," Miranda drawled.

"No, I want to relax her mind. I think she has the wrong impression of what I want. I'm not here to cause her any trouble." He sounded sincere.

"Then by all means, go to her. She's in the bedroom on the left, second door."

"Thanks."

* * *

Darrell didn't knock; he just turned the knob and walked in. Jade was still sleeping. She had never made it under the blanket. Her cell phone was still in her hand. He sat next to her and she didn't move. He could tell she was dreaming. Her eyes were moving from side to side behind her lids.

"Jade," he called softly. When she didn't move, he called her name again, his lips beside her ear. That still didn't wake her. So he kissed her briefly and she rolled her head. He kissed her again and she parted her lips while whispering his name. He looked down at her and knew she was still asleep. He kissed her again, but this time with more intensity. Jade lifted her arms around his neck and pulled his body closer to her. "Darrell," she said, and there was passion in her voice.

"I still love you, Jade. I don't care what your reasons are for taking my son. I just want to be with you and Dee."

Darrell felt Jade release her hold on him. He lifted his body to look into her face. Her light brown eyes were wide-awake. He ran his fingers through her golden brown curls. He lifted her face and a curl that was across her forehead fell back. That's when he noticed the small purple mark on her cheek, and knew he had put it there.

"I'm so sorry for hitting you. I swear, as God as my witness, I'll never put my hands on you again."

Jade remembered what Sheena told her earlier that morning. "I'm going to hold you to that."

"Don't worry, I'm going to love you," he kissed her small rounded nose, "and keep you happy," he kissed her right eye, "make you so satisfied," he kissed her left eye, "that you'll never," he kissed her top lip, "ever," then her bottom lip, "think about leaving me again," then he took her mouth completely in an adoring kiss.

"You're too good for me," she commented meaning exactly what she said.

"You only say that because you don't know your worth," he replied.

She stared at him thinking to herself, *oh boy, if you only knew*. What was going to happen between them? How could she tell him about all the skeletons in her closet? She hadn't told anyone about the real Jade. She continued to stare at him. Her worth? What was she really worth? According to her history, she wasn't worth a cent. And she was tired of pretending that she was.

Soon she would have to let everyone know the truth, the whole truth. The Bible says the truth shall make you free, and she wanted to be free. Nevertheless, this wasn't the time or place. Today Ivy needed her and her focus couldn't be on her dilemma, but Ivy's dilemma. She would handle her own battle at another time. "I need a shower. So can you wait for me in the family room? I promise I won't be long."

"As long as you promise," he smiled at her.

"I do," she answered, sighing in relief.

"Then we'll talk?"

"Not today, Darrell. I really don't need any distractions. I need to concentrate on Ivy and her needs. You understand that, don't you?"

"Yeah, I do. But we really need to handle our business too."

"I know. I promise that you and I will settle everything, but just not right now."

Darrell put his head down for a moment. Jade imagined he was thinking about Dee. She knew he wanted to build a relationship with his son. Even though they could never be together again, there was no way she would keep him from his son. She took her index finger and raised his head to her. His dark gray eyes looked into her light brown ones.

"You can go to Lisa's house and get Dee," she said softly. "He's there with Ivy's kids."

"You want me to bring him back here?"

"No, keep him with you for a while. I'll call Lisa and tell her you're going to pick him up. I know you wanted to take him to your mother's so she can meet him. This will give me time to just be with Ivy and not worry about Dee."

Darrell was grateful she had suggested it without him asking. He stood up and walked toward the door, paused a moment, "We're going to be all right. I know, 'cause I love you just that much." He opened the door and left the room.

Jade bowed her head for a silent prayer asking God to help her let him down easy.

* * *

Ivy had decided early that morning that she needed to be in church and around the saints of God. All the girls decided to accompany her.

When they arrived at the church, the service had already started and the building was crowded. They stood at the middle set of doors, waiting to be ushered down the plush purple-carpeted pathway to Ivy's favorite seat in the second pew.

Pastor Jones noticed his daughter and her friends' entry the moment they stepped in the door. Recognizing that it was standing room-only, he stepped to the podium and announced, "As most of you already know, my daughter lost her husband on Friday evening. And most of you know, she's always on time for morning service. However, today is a difficult one for her and here she is late for the first time in years. I'm going to ask four of you on the first row to give up your seats this morning to my daughter and her friends." You could hear murmurs of *Amen* throughout the congregation and more than four stood to give up their seats. Ushers then placed chairs on the side for the overflow of people.

As always, Pastor James Jones delivered a powerful message about love and how it covers a multitude of sins. It was during that message that Ivy realized it was love that had propelled her to stay with Ray when any ordinary woman would have left him long ago. She was reminded that she was no ordinary woman, but a virtuous woman; and like all people of God, she was a *strange and peculiar* woman, not likely to act or do as the world would expect her to. She was in the world, but not of the world, and because of that reason she would continue to be peculiar to the world.

After hearing her father's words, Ivy stood and made her way to the stairs that led to the platform where the pulpit was. Pastor Jones looked to the ushers who then rushed to her side. She paused for a moment then literally fell to her knees. She lifted her palms in the air as she bowed her head. Tears she couldn't hold back flowed from her eyes like a river.

There wasn't a dry eye in the sanctuary when she wailed, "Lord, please have mercy on me!"

Chapter Eight

As was her custom on Sundays, immediately after morning service, Ivy's mother served a meal fit for a king, one that she had prepared the evening before. Today's Sunday dinner consisted of roast beef, baked macaroni and cheese, collard greens, and sweet potato pie. Everyone enjoyed the feast except Ivy. She couldn't eat a bite.

The other girls tried to get her to take in just enough food to keep her strength up, but Ivy's mood darkened on the drive home when she realized she would be making the final arrangement for Ray's funeral that afternoon.

At Reverend Jones' request, the owner of Thompson's Mortuary came to his house to make the final arrangements for the funeral of his son-in-law. The more details that were finalized, the lower Ivy sank into depression. She could hear the questions, she just didn't know how to respond to them. It was as if they had no grounding in reality. *What about Wednesday, or would you rather have the funeral Thursday or Friday? What about music? What color do you want?* Finally, Ivy instructed the owner to give her whatever was the least expensive. She just wanted it over with as quickly as possible.

So the arrangements were made through her parents. The funeral was set for Wednesday morning, with burial to follow immediately after the service. It was agreed that a representative of Thompson's Mortuary would contact Ray's parents to give them the details of the arrangements.

Ivy moped around the house staring into space for what seemed like hours. Her children were back from Lisa's house, and all the children could sense something was wrong with their mother. Ray Jr. particularly watched her with some concern. It seemed that the reality of his father's death hadn't yet sunk in – after all, Ray had been absent from their home and their lives more often lately than he had been there – and Ray Jr. didn't like the mood his mother was in. It was him that told her, "You need to put an egg in your shoe, Mama, and beat it."

It was good advice. So, Sheena suggested taking Ivy out to get some seafood. Since seafood was her favorite all the girls felt that it might encourage her to eat. Ivy's parents agreed happily to babysit their grandchildren.

* * *

At Club Dazz the band was playing smooth, mellow jazz and the mood was relaxed. Everyone seemed to be enjoying the electric atmosphere surrounding the popular supper club. Sheena, Jade, Miranda, and Ivy had ventured out that evening to escape the drama that surrounded them, if only for a few hours.

The Club Dazz building sat on over half of a city block. It featured two sections, both on the first floor level. The east side of the building was called The Fire Room. No food was served in this section of the establishment. The house dee-jay played the hardcore club music. If someone wanted to party like it was 1999, this was the section to be in, with flashing lights and surround-sound speakers creating the perfect effect for clubbing.

The west side of the building was called Eden. The restaurant featured a huge dining room, decorated in the most elegant silver and gold décor, and was the talk of the town because of its fabulous seafood menu. Sheena recommended this particular place because she found it to be the most upscale establishment in town. She and Jason often had dinner here after working late during the week. Nevertheless, the others felt a bit uncomfortable from the moment they stood outside the building. This was not the type of place they usually frequented.

"I don't know how in the world we allowed Sheena to persuade us to come here tonight," Miranda whispered in Jade's ear.

Ivy looked around the room, and then asked Sheena where the restroom was. Sheena pointed it out, and Jade told her she was going as well.

Miranda looked at Sheena harshly. "Why in the name of God did you bring us to a place like this? This isn't a place for Ivy to be right now, Sheena. What are you thinking?"

"I'm thinking food and entertainment."

"Well, I think we need to get out of here," Miranda commented.

"She needs to eat, doesn't she?" Sheena asked as the waiter came with menus and asked for their drink orders. "Four virgin strawberry daiquiris, please," she ordered. The waiter's eyes lingered on her as he wrote the order down.

"That's all for right now, thank you," Miranda snapped. Without a word, he quickly walked away. Miranda turned her attention back to Sheena.

"I can't believe you. And I can't believe I'm still sittin' here."

"What are we supposed to do, let her starve? She hasn't eaten anything in two days. She's already only a hundred pounds soaking wet."

"That ain't the point, and you know it."

"Look, Ivy loves seafood and they serve the best right here," Sheena protested. "Don't worry, Miranda, it's going to be all right. You won't lose your virtuous status by being here. Pastor Owens comes here all the time."

"Pastor Owens? The same Pastor Owens that got caught checking out of the Red Roof Inn with his church clerk?"

"I don't know anything about that."

"Well, I do. The man is a hypocrite and a disgrace to my grandfather's legacy. I wish he had never ordained that man."

"Now you see, Randi, that's your problem. You're always comparing people to your grandfather and your father. Even if the man had done what you said he did, can't he repent and become whole again?"

"That ain't my point."

"Well, it's mine. So hush up. Here comes Jade."

Halfway through their meal, Miranda looked over at Ivy, already knowing that she wasn't having a particularly good time. Nonetheless, she had pretty

WITHDRAWN

much demolished the lobster tail on her plate, so Sheena had been right about her love of seafood.

Their waiter came back again, for what seemed like the tenth time in the past twenty minutes, asking if they needed anything while his eyes longingly lingered on Sheena.

"Well, I can say one thing," Miranda commented; "the men are still mesmerized by your beauty, Sheena."

"Oh, please, I'm not the only one sitting at this table," she replied.

"Oh, believe me, he's not interested in anyone but you," Miranda said. "All of us have noticed that boyfriend has been over here like what, three times more than average?" Miranda asked. "And he's always looking directly at you."

Ivy looked over at the waiter. "Well, he *is* cute!"

"And young," Jade said.

"Age is just a number," Ivy responded. "You act like she's fifty years old or something. Dang, give a woman a break! He has to be what? Twenty-two or twenty-four years old." Ivy beckoned the waiter to their table.

"Yes, ladies, may I be of service?" There was a wide smile on his face.

"You most certainly may," Ivy said. "Can I have a real strawberry daiquiri and double up on the liquor, please?"

"Ivy!" Miranda gasped.

"You heard the lady," Sheena said to the man.

"What about you, pretty lady?" the waiter asked Sheena seductively.

"I don't drink alcohol," she smiled. "However, I'd love a virgin if you're treating."

The waiter smiled and walked away.

"Well, ain't nobody asked if I wanted one," Miranda complained.

"Yeah, what is this, nobody's here but Sheena and Ivy?" Jade asked, only half-joking.

"Ah, don't be mad at us, Randi," Ivy soothed.

Miranda looked at Sheena. "I can't believe you're condoning what Ivy is doin'."

"Leave her alone. She's in bereavement. Besides, the Bible says and I quote: 'drink thy wine with a merry heart.'" Sheena rolled her eyes at Miranda; and before the other woman could say anything to rebuke her, she started another conversation.

* * *

Jason had been attentive to his date, Janet, the entire evening, even though it took a lot of effort. He had been thinking about Sheena the whole time. He tried his utmost to concentrate on what Janet was saying. The problem was that he wasn't interested in anything she said. He smiled, thinking that being with Sheena never took so much effort. Being with her came naturally. Talking with her was as natural as the winds gently blowing on a warm summer day.

Now he knew he was losing it. The woman he just glanced at across the room looked just like Sheena. But no, it couldn't be; she would never patronize this place without him. He focused on what he thought was an illusion and realized that it wasn't. Jade, Miranda, Ivy, and Sheena were all here. He continued to watch them having what seemed to be a good time.

He couldn't believe that Ivy was out. Her husband had just passed away, and here she was, just living it up! Janet noticed that his attention was focused across the room, and she began to stare at him. His nostrils flared while he watched the waiter, who was hanging around the table, flirting with the ladies.

"Jason, what's wrong?" Janet asked finally, trying to get his attention back to her.

"Nothing, are you ready to go?" He asked it with a little more snap than he intended. Janet looked over at the table where he had focused his attention, and noticed that the waiter had sat down next to the light-skinned woman.

Jason was totally absorbed with the activity going on at that table, and it unnerved her. "I assume it's someone you know?" she asked. He never answered her question. He just continued to watch them. A few more moments passed with his concentration engulfed in watching them.

Janet called his name three times but Jason never acknowledged her. The next time she called his name more forcefully and tapped him on the shoulder.

Jason turned toward her and answered slowly, "Yeah."

"Is it her?"

"Her?" he asked, a little confused as to what she meant.

"The one that keeps me from being more than a booty call?"

Before Jason could answer, Jade waved hi to him. He acknowledged her by a nod of his head. Janet got up. "Come on, I want to meet her."

Before Jason could object, Janet pulled him up and approached their table.

"Hello," they all said, practically in unison.

"Have you had dinner yet?" Ivy asked.

"Yeah, we were about to leave," he answered, not taking his eyes off Sheena.

"Jason, introduce us to your friend," Jade said.

Jason looked uncomfortable. "Everyone, this is Janet Brown."

"Hi, Janet," Ivy greeted, extending her hand. "This is my cousin Miranda Jones and my sisters in spirit and very good friends, Jade Sanders and Sheena Daniels."

"So nice to meet you all," Janet said, greeting Jade first. She then turned to Sheena and knew immediately that she was the one that held Jason's attention. If beauty had a picture, it would definitely be Sheena Daniels. *The woman could model for Vogue magazine*, Janet thought. She knew she had stared too long when one of the other women cleared her throat. She looked around, embarrassed at her action. "I'm sorry, I didn't mean... Forgive me," she stammered.

"Don't worry about it," Ivy said, a slur beginning to show in her voice. "Sheena has that effect on everyone. She's used to being stared at."

Jade laughed. "Yeah, it gets us a lot of free drinks too, doesn't it, Sheena?"

"Do you model or…?"

"No, I don't." Sheena answered a little too quickly.

"Sheen, look, there's Pastor Owens," Miranda said, drawing her attention away from Janet.

Janet tilted her head away from Sheena to address Jason. "This is your Sheen?" Sheen is Sheena?" she asked, looking for confirmation. "You work with…" she cut off her statement. "Ooh!" she said, with an awkward expression on her face. "So you are the Sheen I've heard so much about?" Knowing without confirmation, Janet continued, "I thought you were a guy. Jason talks about you all the time. Well, I should have known. There's no way a male could take up that much of his time or mind."

"Sit down with us and chat a while, Jason," Jade offered, now even more interested in this Janet woman.

"No, we were just leaving." He looked over at Sheena who was staring right back at him.

"We can stay a little while with your friends, honey," said Janet. "Let's sit down." She pulled out a chair, looked over at Jade, and with a wave of her manicured hand she said, "He's just anxious to get me tucked in for the night." Then she turned to look at Sheena. "I'm sure you can understand that."

"Why would I understand that?" Sheena's voice was dangerously steady.

Jason heard the venom and knew it was time to leave. "Let's go, Janet," he said before she could sit down comfortably. "I mean right now."

"Damn, Jason. Was it something I said?" Janet asked.

Jason ignored her. "Goodnight, everyone."

Sheena was the only one who didn't respond.

Chapter Nine

Sheena was furious. She couldn't believe that Jason had escorted one of his women to Club Dazz – not only that, he had allowed that woman to blatantly disrespect her! And this was the same man who had been declaring his undying love for her just yesterday?

"Sheena, no one said you'd done anything. Why are you so upset?" Ivy asked. "You've been talking about that woman – what's her name again?"

"Janet," Miranda supplied helpfully.

"Yeah, Janet, ever since we left Club Dazz. Dang, girl, give it a rest!"

"You know what I'm upset about?" Sheena asked, not waiting for an answer. "I'm pissed because she implied that I've slept with him."

"Sheena, the woman is ignorant. You just have to overlook people like her," Ivy replied. Everyone could hear now that she was slurring her words. She had problems inserting her key in the front door. Miranda took it from her without a word and unlocked the door, letting them all inside.

"Well, the whole thing was interesting to me," Jade said, tossing her purse on a chair. "In fact, I rather enjoyed it. Other people's dramas are always more interesting than your own."

"Oh, I was fine, too, until Miss Thang got in my space," Sheena huffed. "You wait until I see Jason again. I've got something for his behind."

"Dang, girl, she was jealous, Sheena, couldn't you see that?"

"Jealous of what? She was there with him, not me. She's the one he's tucking in right now, probably as we speak, not me."

"You're gorgeous, girl. From the time they stepped foot near our table, not only did her eyes bulge from her head, but Jason couldn't keep his eyes off you," Ivy stumbled onto the sofa.

"I think you've had just a little too much to drink." Miranda observed.

"What are you saying? That I'm drunk? Well if I am, that's fine, 'cause I'm feeling real good right about now. Hell, turn some music on. Whew!" she said, snapping her fingers.

"Oh, yeah, she's definitely drunk," Miranda stated matter-of-factly to the room at large, nodding knowingly.

Ivy giggled. "Let's not talk about Jason. Let's not talk about Darrell. And, whatever you do, please don't talk about Ray. Let's not even talk about me being drunk. Let's just chill out. I still have some of that sparkling apple cider that Mama brought us. And I have those 1970 flicks I picked out especially for this weekend.

Here, look at what I have. There's *Super Fly, Foxy Brown, Claudine…*"

"You have *Claudine*? The one with James Earl Jones in it? Jade's voice was eager.

"That's the one."

"*Oh, keep away from me, Mr. Welfare,*" they all sang in unison.

"They sure knew how to make a black movie back in the 70s, girl!" Miranda laughed.

"They sure did."

"All right, now," Ivy slurred. "*Claudine* it is."

* * *

Ivy heard a ringing sound in her ears. It was extremely loud. When she opened her eyes, she quickly closed them again. The light was painful. There it was again, the ringing. Ivy attempted to raise her head from the sofa, but when she did, the room began to spin. She peeped out of one eye and noticed all the girls still in the family room, each taking up a space on the surrounding sectional. She heard Miranda ask if she wanted her to get the door.

"Yes, please, my head is killing me."

"Serves you right, drinking like you did last night," Miranda replied.

"Just get the door, rug-rat."

In just a few minutes Miranda returned and announced that it was Bill Hart, Ray's attorney, to see her. Ivy was not prepared to deal with her ongoing drama yet. Not until she had had some aspirin, at least. She told Miranda to tell him to call her later and make arrangements to see her.

"You should see what the man wants," Jade's voice piped up from someplace nearby. Ivy didn't open her eyes again to check out where she was. Everything felt much better with her eyes closed.

"Whatever he's here for can't be good," she said, "and I'm not feeling well enough to stomach any mess this morning. If Ray left everything to his mother, then I'm sure he's representing them now."

"Well, you really don't know anything until you communicate with the man," Sheena chimed in.

"It doesn't make me any difference. My head is hurting, my stomach is sour, and I feel like crap. I don't want to deal with any bull this morning."

"Actually, it's not really morning. It's more like noon," Jade replied. She sounded far too cheerful.

"Why didn't he just call, anyway?" Ivy finally sat up, putting her hand over her stomach. *If I haven't thrown up by now, I probably won't*, she was thinking.

"Well, I can answer that one! Bigfoot over there kicked the phone off the hook," Sheena replied, pointing at Jade.

"Who, me?"

"Yes, you. I started to wake your silly behind up. You called Darrell's name mostly all night."

"You're joking, right?"

Sheena's face was serious. "Am I laughing?"

Miranda stepped back into the room. "Okay, I got rid of him. But he told me to tell you that if you needed anything, anything at all, to call him. I told him you weren't feeling too well."

"Thanks, Randi."

"Bill told me that mostly all Ray's friends are visiting his parents' house and sending condolences there."

"Well, that's not all that surprising," Ivy nodded, forgetting how much it hurt to move.

Miranda arched her eyebrows "Why would you think that?"

Ivy shrugged. "They're his parents."

Miranda sucked her teeth. "But he lived here with you! You were his wife!"

"Most of his friends knew we weren't getting along," Ivy rubbed her eyes, wishing the jackhammers in her head would leave her alone.

"Well, Bill told me everyone has been told that everything will be taking place from Ray's parents' home, not here. The man thought you would be over there since that's where everything's supposed to be. He said when he asked about you, Ray's parents brushed him off. Then someone told him you hadn't been there at all."

"So I thought right; everyone's going to her house," Ivy said, finally understanding why no one had come or even called her with condolences. "That manipulative witch. I was thinking no one cared about me at all."

Miranda shrugged. "Well, anyway, I told him what a hard time they been givin' you. He said he'd give you a call in a few hours and if you wanted him to straighten everything out for you, just let him know."

"See, girl, I told you that you should have talked to the man," Jade interjected.

Abruptly, Ivy stood up, held her stomach, looked over at her friends, and rushed to the bathroom like a bat out of hell.

* * *

Ivy's parents arrived at her house early that afternoon with her children in tow. A few hours previously, the infamous Reverend Owens had seen the Reverend and Mrs. Jones with their grandchildren having breakfast at the IHOP, where he told them that he had seen the girls at Club Dazz the night before.

Ivy's father was appalled. In his wildest imagination, he never would have thought that his daughter and his niece would go to a place like Club Dazz, especially with Ivy supposedly in mourning. That, he said to his wife, was not why they had agreed to babysit. That was not why they had agreed to help her. *Ivy at Club Dazz?*

When they pulled into the driveway, the couple noticed the extra cars and identified each except the gray Volvo. Little Ray knew it immediately and told his grandparents that it belonged to his father's mother.

They could tell before they reached the family room that an argument was in progress.

"You are hateful, as well as inconsiderate," Anna Miller was saying, all the while wagging her finger two inches from her daughter-in-law's face. "You didn't even ask me if Wednesday would be all right for my son's funeral. Most of my family can't even get here until the weekend, and you made those arrangements to spite me!"

Ivy looked at her mother-in-law. She told herself she wasn't going to cry anymore. This woman had always treated her like she was insignificant.

But the animosity between them hadn't always been there.

Ivy had been in the fourth grade when Ray and his family moved in next door. Ray was larger than most kids his age, so when Ivy first saw him, she thought he was fourteen or fifteen years old. Ivy was smitten from the very beginning.

What she didn't know then was that Ray had his eye on her, too. It was her hair that had attracted him. Ivy's ponytail was long enough for her to sit on. Ray and his brother ogled her as she sat on the front porch with two other girls, playing jacks.

"You think her hair is real, Pete?" Ray asked his twelve-year-old brother.

"No, that ain't her real hair. Ain't no black girls got hair that long. Don't you remember grandma had that long plait in her room that she used to put on her head and twist it like a snake on the top?

"Yeah."

"Well, that's what it is. She just doesn't twist hers, that's all."

"It looks real to me."

"Want to make a bet it's not real?

Ten-year-old Ray looked over at Ivy and she smiled at him. He did the natural thing and smiled back. Not taking his eyes off her, he said to his brother, "Okay, I'll bet you it's real and if I win, she's my girlfriend. And if you win, she's your girlfriend."

Peter laughed as he said, "If I win or not, she's gonna be my girlfriend, 'cause I can tell she don't like fat boys."

"I'm not fat, you just skinny. I'm goin' over there and ask her."

"No, Ray, you just can't go over there and ask the girl if her hair's real."

"How else am I gonna find out?"

Pete considered the question and came up with an answer. "We wait a few days and ask her friends or something."

"No, I want to know now."

Ray started toward Ivy's porch. Peter called to him, but Ray ignored his brother. "Hi," he said to the girls as he approached. "My name is Ray and that's my brother Pete over there."

"Hi, Ray!" She smiled warmly. "My name's Ivy and this is my cousin Randi and this is Sheena." They didn't stop looking at each other and the girls snickered.

Ray licked his lips. "Can I ask you something?"

"Sure," Ivy answered.

"Is that your real hair?" Ivy didn't answer at first, and the other girls snickered even louder. "My brother said it's not real. I told him that it was, and he bet me that it wasn't."

Without saying a word, Ivy began to unbind her hair. Ray stared at her in amazement, and when she completed the task she ran her fingers through her tresses and told Ray to do the same.

"It's real, it's real," he hollered out loudly to his brother who was standing in awe. "I told you, I told you," Ray shouted in victory. He turned back to Ivy. "Can I ask you another question?"

"Sure," Ivy answered with a smile.

"How old are you?"

"I'm nine, but I'll be ten next week."

"Well, I'm ten already and I'll be eleven in December."

She glanced at her friends. "We were wondering how old you were. We thought you were a lot older."

"That's because I'm a football player. You have to be big and strong to be a world champ."

"Yeah, I guess so."

"Can I ask you one more question?"

"Okay."

"Will you be my girlfriend?"

"We don't even know each other!"

"That's okay, we'll get to know each other while you're my girl."

"Okay."

Ray noticed his mother standing at the door. Impulsively, he took Ivy by the hand and pulled her over to where his mother stood.

"Mom, look, I made a friend already."

"See? I told you you would," she said to Ray. "Hello, I'm your new friend's mother. Mrs. Miller. What's your name, sweetie?"

"Ivy Jones."

"Oh, you wouldn't happen to be related to Pastor Jones at Cathedral, would you?"

"Yes ma'am, he's my grandfather," Ivy said proudly.

"Well, you be sure to come visit us after we get all moved in, you hear?"

"Yes, ma'am, I will."

Ray said, "She lives right next door, Mom."

"Is that so? Well, I'm sure we're going to be good friends, then."

That was then, Ivy thought sadly. This is now.

"Earth to Ivy, earth to Ivy. Do you hear what I'm telling you? You're not even listening to me," Ray's mother ranted. "You need to have a wake on Friday and have the funeral on Saturday; and you need to change it right now while I'm here."

"I'm not changing anything. Whoever wants to be here will just have to arrange their schedules so they can."

"Are you deaf? I said these people are from out of town. It takes time to get from Texas to New Jersey. I need you to change that date."

"Anna!" Ivy's mother called as she and her husband stepped into the room. "Get your hand out of my daughter's face!" Patricia's voice was lethal. Everyone in the room – Anna, Miranda, Ivy, Sheena, and Jade – froze when they heard her tone. She used it infrequently and effectively. "Now, you listen to me. Ivy doesn't want to have the funeral over the weekend. As mother to his children, she's doing what's best for her immediate family and you need to recognize and respect that."

The twin girls rushed toward their mother. Ivy picked one up and the other held on to her leg.

"All of you Joneses are alike." Anna observed the girls clinging to their mother protectively nevertheless, she pressed with her attack. "You're selfish and inconsiderate of other people." Ray Jr. rested against the chair watching his grandmothers with scrutiny and Anna knew it.

"Give her to me, Ivy." Miranda took the child Ivy was holding and sat her on the sectional sofa. Jade picked up the other girl and placed her beside her identical twin.

Anna's eyes followed Solomon as he positioned himself next to his mother. She focused her attention on Patricia. "That's why I left your church."

Patricia was having none of it. "Anna, you left the church because you couldn't run things. You brought more confusion than any member we ever had at Cathedral of Faith. You single-handedly drove the Childs family out of the church just because their fifteen-year-old daughter got pregnant, and instead of praying for the situation you had to run them down by running your mouth."

"Well, Pastor Owens is glad to have me."

"I'm glad you found a church home that fits you, Anna. Satan is the author of confusion, and I'm sure being there with Pastor Owens, you've found your place."

Anna's mouth dropped open and Patricia knew she couldn't wait to tell her pastor what she just said.

"Oh, Anna?" Reverend Jones threw in, "Before you run and tell Owens what my wife just said, you be sure to let your family know that the arrangements stand as they are. So whoever is not there the day after tomorrow won't be able to pay their last respects. Now, dear lady, you are dismissed. I won't have you upsetting my daughter any more, for as long as I live on this earth."

Anna looked around the room at each of them. Her eyes lingered on the faces of her grandchildren who were watching her intently. Ray Junior, to whom she hadn't paid much attention over the years, had turned into a handsome young man. He was tall for his age, just as her son had been; and he resembled his father as well. She didn't want to act foolish in front of the children, and the fact that she was outnumbered made her think twice about arguing further. After rolling her eyes at Ivy, she swung around and headed to the front door without uttering another word.

Ivy hugged her mother. "Thank you, Mama." She was relieved. She turned to her father, opened her arms thanking him with a hug too. "She just marched in here and called me everything but a child of God."

"Junior, take your brother and sisters to your room and watch television," the Reverend Jones directed.

Ivy waited for the children to leave the room before she said, "I guess I should have considered the rest of Ray's family. They *are* a large group."

Her mother shook her head. "If her relationship with you was what it should be, that conversation would never have taken place. I think getting it over with as quickly as possible is best for you. Especially after what your father and I just heard from Pastor Owens."

Ivy's dad knitted his brows and looked around the room. "Yes, I understand you girls went over to Dazz and had a party."

"Now, you see, that's a lie," Miranda protested. "We went there for food, not to party. The section we were in was for dining. You know better than to listen to

Reverend Owens. That's why I can't stand that man. He's a liar straight from hell. "

"That may be so, but you girls know better. You should have had take-out instead."

"You're right, Pastor. We should have," Jade agreed, and the others nodded.

Chapter Ten

It wasn't over yet. Ivy, Miranda, Jade, and Sheena had to endure a private sermon on Romans, chapter fourteen, verses sixteen and seventeen: "Let not then your good be evil spoken of: For the kingdom of God is not *meat and drink*, but righteousness, and peace, and joy in the Holy Ghost." After Reverend Jones preached his fifteen-minute sermon, Ivy's mother sent them to the car to retrieve the food that members of the church had prepared for the bereaved family.

Soon after that, Lisa and John arrived, and all of them – except Ivy – enjoyed the meal as they reminisced about the good times shared with Ray. After they finished telling stories about the good old days, and the children had gone to their rooms, Ivy's father turned to her with a concerned look on his face. "You didn't eat anything, baby."

"I know, Daddy. I just don't have an appetite. Besides, my stomach is paying the price for what I consumed last night."

"Well, I pray you've learned your lesson."

"Yeah, I learned it well."

He father paused. "He came to see me the week before the accident."

"Who, Ray?" Ivy was startled.

"Yeah. He said he wanted to apologize for not keeping his promise."

"What promise?"

"To love, honor, and cherish you," her father answered, looking directly into his daughter's eyes.

She felt a flutter in her stomach, but quelled it. "That's nice, Daddy. But he should have been apologizing to me, not you!"

"In his own way, he was apologizing to you."

"Talking to you was apologizing to me? What did he ask you to do, be his messenger?" Ivy knew she was getting angry. Every time she thought about something that had happened over the past year, she became downright hostile. She had a lot of pain to get over.

"Ivy, you're going to have to really put that bitterness away. I know if Ray had known what he was doing – and I mean *really* knew what he was doing, not only to you and the children, but to himself – he would never have done it. I know he loved you, Ivy. The man had tears in his eyes when he told me that you wanted a divorce."

"He told you that?" she asked rhetorically, knowing if her father said it, Ray had indeed gone to him with his side of the story.

"Yeah, he told me."

Ivy's mother was staring at her husband. "James, you never said anything to me. I didn't know until Ivy told me."

"I know I didn't, Pat. I really believed that everything was going to work out between the two of them, and that I would never have to tell you about our conversation."

"Well, it has worked out," Ivy stated matter-of-factly. "He's gone, so I can truly say it was until death do us part." There were eight people in the room, yet suddenly a hush fell over them all. Into the silence, Ivy said, "He wanted that divorce, not me. He just stopped loving me." She forced herself to hold back the tears. "Daddy..."

"Yeah."

"Did he tell you that he told me to do what I had to do, and that it didn't make any difference to him that I still wanted him, and that I needed to do him and me a favor and just divorce him?"

"Yes, he told me he said that. But he didn't mean it."

Ivy was blown away. She knew that her father would not lie to her, not even to save her feelings. "Well, he said it like he meant it." She rolled her eyes to the ceiling. "If he didn't want me, fine. All he had to do was take care of his children. He wouldn't even do that. He knew we spent everything we had to help him, and what thanks did I get?"

"He said he was allowing you to divorce him so..."

"Allowing me?" Ivy exclaimed, interrupting her father.

"Yes, allowing you. And now that I think back on it, I'm beginning to feel that he knew he wasn't going to be here long."

"Why is that?" Jade asked, perplexed.

"Well, let me tell you exactly what happened the day he came to see me."

One week earlier...

Ivy's father had been in his study for hours, working on the following week's sermon when his wife tapped lightly on the door to notify him that Ray was there and needed to speak with him. Lord knew he had been praying for his son-in-law to come to him on his own without being coached to do so!

In his heart, the pastor felt that once Ray was sick and tired of being sick and tired of his addiction, then – and only then – could God step in and begin the process of restoring him to his full potential by transmogrifying him from the inside out. He knew there was something magnificent deep inside of the younger man and his prayer was to witness him becoming all that God intended him to be.

The conversation was certainly not an answer to the pastor's prayers. In fact, it was one that he never dreamed he would have to have with his daughter's husband.

It was when the word divorce came from his son-in-law's lips that he realized the marriage was no longer redeemable. In the history of his family, as far back as he could remember, no one had ever gotten a divorce. He believed in *for better or for worse, in sickness and in health*. Ray was definitely sick. So why would his daughter fix her mouth to even ask her husband of eleven years for a divorce?

As if Ray could read his thoughts, he said, "Don't blame Ivy for walking away from our marriage, Dad. She's taken more than she should have, more than I thought she would, and more than any other woman would have. Every penny I get goes into my habit, and the only way I'm going to take care of my responsibilities is for her to take what is hers by divorcing me."

"Ray, if you know it's wrong, why do you continue to do it?"

"Don't you think if I *could* stop, I would have, a long time ago?" he asked, desperation in his voice. Putting his head down, he searched for the right words to say. "I never thought I would hurt my family the way I have. I never envisioned that I'd be dependant on anything but God, but this demon is bigger than my faith in Him."

"Son, you can beat this thing…"

"Dad, I've been there, done that. I don't have to tell you. I can't win and I want Ivy to do this for the sake of our children. You see, I know that it's over for me, Dad. I'm just trying to get my affairs in order. I'm not Hezekiah, who turned his face to the wall and prayed to God, saying how he walked before him in truth with a perfect heart and did good in his sight, and because of that his life was extended another fifteen years. Well, that's not gonna happen for me. I'm going to reap what I sowed. I know how you feel about divorce, but there comes a time when it's necessary. So I'm begging you not to fight her when she tells you. Support her and be there for her. Allow her to cry on your shoulder and let her know that God's got her back and He always will." He hesitated. "And please, Dad, pray for me. Ask God to have mercy on my soul."

"Ray, if you stop right now and allow me to put you into treatment, I promise you, son, this…"

"No."

"You're talking crazy, boy. Don't you know your children need you and that…"

"Dad, I know what I have to do. As for my children, they're going to be just fine. I know this because you're their grandfather." Ray stared at him as if to say, *now tell me I'm wrong.*

"Well, I see you have your mind made up so there's nothing more for me to say."

Ray walked to Reverend Jones' office door and, just before he walked out, he turned back to his father-in-law and said, "I still love her, Dad. No matter what she may think or what she says to you, I still love her. I always have, and I always will."

* * *

Now, in Ivy's dining-room, Reverend Jones paused before saying in a soothing voice, "That was the last conversation I had with Ray. It was just over a week ago. Now, I don't know if he was aware of it or not, but the boy's eyes were glassy when he was talking to me. I didn't see a tear drop, but I do believe that after he walked out that door and got into his car, a tear or two fell from his eyes, probably even more."

"Ivy, Bill is here again." Ivy had been so wrapped up in her father's story that she never heard the doorbell. "He said he knows you told him to call first, but he was in the neighborhood and…"

"Let him in, Randi, it's okay," she instructed even through she was suspicious of the lawyer's intentions. "Let's go sit in the family room, okay? We can clean all this dinner stuff up after he leaves."

Bill Hart entered the room and greeted everyone. He asked to speak to Ivy alone. Her first thought was to decline. Whatever he wanted to say should be able to be said in front of everyone; but she noticed that he had been looking at Lisa, and when he turned to face her again his eyes held what he did not say with words, *please, Ivy?*

Patricia said, "You go on and handle your business. We'll go and do the dishes."

Ivy directed Bill to the sun porch located directly behind the kitchen, which afforded them full privacy once the French doors were closed. She gestured with her hand toward the group of patio chairs and asked Bill to have a seat. After he did, she continued to stand, folding her arms across her chest and giving him her full attention.

"Why don't you sit down, Ivy?"

"I'd rather stand, thank you."

"Okay. First of all, I wanted to ask you if you need anything."

"No, I'm all right."

"Are you sure? I understand that you're under a financial strain."

"Oh, really, what gave you that idea?" she asked sarcastically.

"Look, Ivy, I know you're still upset with me about not filing the divorce papers for you."

"No, Bill, that's not so. I understand your position."

"Then why do I sense hostility between us?"

"I don't know. Maybe it's because my feelings are hurt, and I don't know who to trust anymore."

Bill stretched his arm across the chair, took a deep breath, and then relaxed. "Actually, Ray gave me that idea."

"What?" Ivy asked, perplexed.

"You asked who gave me the idea that you were financially strained. Well, I'm telling you, Ray did."

Ivy lifted an eyebrow in curiosity. "When?"

"He came to me just a few days before the accident and asked me to help him help you."

Now he had Ivy's full attention. "What are you saying?"

"He knew you were hurting. He hated himself for what you were going through. He instructed me to arrange for you to receive half of his pension. When he told me about the house being at risk of foreclosure, I took it upon myself to contact the mortgage company to make the back payments. As of last Friday, your mortgage is paid up."

Feeling light-headed, Ivy sat down in a chair across from Bill. "I really appreciate that. But I won't be able to make the payments, so I'll have to sell the house anyway."

Bill tilted his head to one side, "No, you won't." He got up, walked over to the window, and looked out as if he was admiring the scenery. "Like I said, your mortgage is paid up." He put his hands in his pockets.

"What are you saying, Bill?" Ivy asked in confusion.

"When Ray died, the life insurance policy that was included in your monthly mortgage payment paid it off. So you don't have to disrupt the children's lives anymore than they already are. The house is yours."

Ivy moved her eyes from his and focused on the lapel on his suit jacket. The room was completely quiet for a short time. Ivy turned her back from him as she thought about what her father had told her, just moments before Bill's arrival. What Bill was telling her now only confirmed what her father had said earlier. Could it be that Ray had provoked her purposely to file for a divorce? In his own way, was he trying to protect her? Her mind was spinning. Now she had more than just a few questions to which she needed answers.

The most important one could not be answered by anyone other than Ray himself. Knowing that to be a fact, she turned her attention back to Bill and asked him the question she felt only Ray could answer anyway. "Did he still love me, Bill?"

Without hesitation he answered, "Without a doubt in my mind, I can honestly say that he loved you, Ivy."

"Then how could he treat me so, so…"

"He told me a few months ago that you would give up everything you had and be willing to live in public housing just to help him become whole again.

"Because I loved him."

"He knew that. That's why he told me to lie to you about certain things, such as him selling the house in Florida and cashing in the 401(k). He said that you would have liquidated everything to see that he received the best treatment possible."

"He still has the house?"

"Yes, *you* still have the house. I've been renting it out as a vacation home for the past year. It's been making a few thousand a month. "

Ivy couldn't believe her ears, and now she was totally speechless.

"Look, I'm not at liberty to talk freely at this time. Since you're having the funeral on Wednesday, I can set up a reading of his will on Friday if you'd like."

"I didn't think he had anything to leave anyone."

"Well, you were wrong about that. He just didn't want you to know about all he really had."

"So he let me believe that he had thrown away thousands of dollars on drugs?"

"Yes, he did, just so you wouldn't spend it on him."

"I don't understand. If he didn't want to go into treatment, why didn't he just say so?"

"He did. He said it a lot. You just didn't want to hear it. You wanted him well, and at first he tried just for you. When you started investing in all those treatment programs, you began to spend more than he did on his habit and he didn't want you to do it. And you weren't ready to hear what he really needed."

"I would rather work two jobs and have him here with me free from dependencies than to have him... Oh, God..."

She had promised herself that she wouldn't cry any more. But suddenly she was in Bill's arms, unable to control the flow of tears. She wept for her children, she wept because she had lost the only man she ever loved, and she wept because she failed to understand him enough to save him.

She had been blaming him for everything. But when a marriage breaks down, there is always enough blame to go around. *What if I had been willing to listen to him? Really, really listen?*

Bill let her cry, wrapped in his arms with her face in his chest, until she was spent. He stroked her back and with the gentlest voice he could muster, assured her that everything was going to be all right.

After a while, she moved away from him and apologized. "Forgive me. I thought I had more control."

Bill removed a monogrammed handkerchief from the inside pocket of his jacket and handed it to Ivy.

"Thank you." She was embarrassed and turned her back to him.

"It's all right, Ivy. What you're feeling is to be expected. I understand."

Ivy sniffled. "Is it essential for me to be with his parents when the will is read?"

Bill could only look at her back, at the long dark plait of hair that Ray had so loved hanging down between her shoulders. "I'm afraid so. He stipulated that he wanted it read within forty-eight hours of his burial. The reason why, I think, is for there to be closure for all concerned parties as quickly as possible."

"Well then, ten o'clock Friday morning would be a good time for me." She turned to face him. "I won't come alone, though. I need some support."

"Understood. Now, do you need anything at the moment?"

Ivy gave him a half-smile. "Actually, there is. I need to change some of the arrangements I made for the funeral. You see, I got the most inexpensive…"

"Say no more. Give the director a call, and let them know that I'll be making some changes."

"You don't think it's too late?"

"Money talks. Do you want anything special?"

"No, I just want him buried nicely."

"You got it."

Ivy held up Bill's handkerchief, "I'll clean this and give it back to you."

"No, you keep it just in case you need it again."

Chapter Eleven

A steady flow of visitors came to the house the evening before Ray's funeral. Virtually everyone apologized for not coming to her sooner with his or her condolences. Ivy knew it was because Ray's parents had told everyone that they were handling all of the arrangements, so naturally people thought she would be there with his parents.

Members of the NFL Alumni began to phone in from all over the country. Hearing from so many of them made Ivy think of some of the best years that she and Ray had shared together.

When the florist called to inform her that she had a truck full of flowers to be delivered, Ivy was perplexed. Bill was there, though, and he took care of everything. An hour after he left her house, he sent his assistant to her so that she could review and approve the official press release. After reading it, Ivy signed her consent for release.

The assistant informed her that she was there to be at Ivy's beck and call. Ivy was grateful, though she refused the service. After the assistant left, Ivy sat in her living room with a copy of the press release in her hand and began reading it again, this time more carefully.

Former NFL defensive star Raymond Terrell Miller, who played with the Dallas Cowboys and the Washington Redskins, died Friday at age of thirty. The four-time NFL Defensive Player of the year was also a licensed minister.

Miller passed away at Cooper Medical Center in Camden, New Jersey, from injuries sustained in an automobile accident on Route 70 in Cherry Hill, New Jersey. The 6' 4" 275-pound player had five consecutive pro bowls and retired as third all-time NFL leaders in sacks.

Ray, as he was called by family and friends, set up a youth community center, naming it the Ray Miller Youth Build Center. The center specializes in counseling services and various athletic activities such as the Ivy Youth Bowling League, named for his wife.

Miller leaves behind his wife of eleven years, Ivy Jones-Miller; two sons, Raymond Jr. and Solomon; and twin daughters, Tamara and Terra. In addition to his wife and children, he also leaves his parents, Mr. & Mrs. Carson Raymond Miller, an older brother Peter Miller, a sister, Lisa Miller, and a host of in-laws, nieces, nephews, cousins, and friends. A public visitation will be held for Ray Miller from 8:00 a.m. to 1 p.m. tomorrow at the Cathedral Of Faith Christian Center. A private funeral will follow.

The family asks that in lieu of flowers, donations be made to The Raymond Terrell Miller's Foundation, P.O. Box 12370, Federal Street, Camden, NJ 08100.

Ivy took a deep breath. Hearing the words made them become real, more painful than she could have imagined. Hearing the words, more than anything else, convinced her that Ray was dead.

As Ivy looked around the room, her eyes fell on various groups of people sitting around chatting. Even with all these people in the house, she felt alone. She was feeling lost now, more so than ever, since this nightmare began. She realized at that moment that life was short, and no one ever knows when it will be their last day on this earth.

Ivy felt the need to be isolated from the crowd, so she went to her bedroom, closed the door, and sat on the edge of her bed. She wanted to cry, yet not a tear would fall from her eyes. After sitting there for a time, she heard a light knock on her door. When she didn't answer, Miranda pushed the door open.

"Did you say come in and I didn't hear you?"

Ivy simply rolled her eyes at her cousin. Then she noticed Miranda hadn't come alone; Jade was standing there with her.

"You need to eat something." Jade was trying to give her a plate of food.

"I don't want it, Jade."

"Look, Ivy, you have to eat something. Now, don't give me a hard time or I'll have to use the funnel and force-feed you."

"I'll try and eat before the night is over, I promise. Just not now, okay?"

"Okay." She called to Ivy's son, Ray Junior, to take the plate back into the kitchen. Miranda stood near the window and Jade sat on the bed next to Ivy, took her hand and said, "It's beginning to sink in that he's really gone, isn't it?"

"Yeah, too real. How many times do I have to say thank you or yes he will be missed?"

"As many times as you have to. I'm just happy to see the flow of people showing that they do care about you."

"They cared about Ray, Jade, not me." She took a deep breath. "And that's what's really important, you know? I'm just realizing how much he's done for the community. The number of kids he supported through the center is enormous. They loved him and I'm... I'm feeling numb right now. I need to eulogize my husband tomorrow, and I'm so out of sync with what everyone else sees in him, that I'm afraid to say anything. They looked at him like a hero and I knew the real Ray Miller, with all his imperfections and shortcomings. And you know what else?

"What?"

"I just realized that not many people knew about his addiction. I'm wondering if they knew about his other women."

"Other women or one particular woman?" Miranda probed gently.

"My guess is everyone knew about her. I'm the one who just found out a few months ago," Ivy answered, saddened by the truth.

Jade shook her head. "Were you hearing your father today? I mean, really hearing him? Ray loved the ground you walked on, girl. Those other wenches can't even compete with you. Please!"

"Oh, that was to save face. Believe me, he respected my father more than he respected me."

"Look, girl, your father is no fool."

"No, he's not, but he was blind to Ray's charm and he believed whatever Ray told him."

"Oh, Ivy, you know you're exaggerating the truth," Miranda was shaking her head.

"Now, you know as well as I do that Ray has had Daddy wrapped around his finger since the beginning, Randi. You remember the Fourth of July barbeque when Ray told our families that we were getting married?"

"I wasn't there but I heard about Ray's mother acting crazy and Aunt Pat almost knocking her out!"

"Well, what you all didn't know was the conversation Ray and I had earlier that morning."

* * *

It was the summer following Ray and Ivy's high school graduation that Ray decided to take a stand and do exactly what he wanted to do – which was to marry Ivy. Both of their families agreed that the young couple should wait until they completed college before entering into holy matrimony.

It was a quarter to six in the morning on that hot July day when Ray called Ivy on her bedroom's private line, asking her to get dressed and meet him on her back porch.

Ivy was half-asleep when she first spoke with him. She listened to him, hung up the phone, and then lay her head back on her pillow, going back to sleep.

After hanging up the phone, Ray went out his back door, hopped over the fence that separated their yards, and waited for Ivy at her back door. When she didn't come in what he thought was a reasonable time, Ray put his finger in his mouth and whistled the code they have been using for years, signaling that he was there.

Ivy heard him and looked outside her window. Ray beckoned with his hand.

Ivy rushed to the hallway bathroom as quietly as she could, brushed her teeth, and washed her face. She was dressed in five minutes. She eased past her parents' bedroom and slid down the banister to avoid stepping on the stairs that always squeaked. After gently opening the back door and stepping past the threshold, Ray took her by the arm, pulling her to his chest and kissing her more passionately than he ever had before. Ivy liked the kiss just a little too much. She knew that to be a fact, because she became weak in the knees. She thanked God that Ray was holding her tightly, because if he hadn't been, she would have surely fallen.

She pulled herself together, realizing that it was more than just a kiss. Ray was branding her and entering her very soul. She pulled away from him and stared up into his beautiful brown eyes.

Ray was not a handsome man. Even as a young boy, he was rugged-looking. Right now he was looking serious, and when he was serious, he looked mean. But his eyes always told the real story. His eyes were definitely the windows to his soul. He had the most beautiful eyes Ivy had ever seen, and to her he was gorgeous.

After he gave no explanation for why he had come to her so early in the morning, she began to guess at the reason.

"What's wrong, Ray? Did your father threaten to leave your mother again?"

"No," he answered softly.

"Oh, God, did your father find out you took his car last night?"

"No."

Ivy looked at him as she widened her eyes in surprise. "Oh no, they found out about the speeding ticket?"

"No, Ivy," he said with just a little more force.

Ivy was frustrated. "Then what is it?"

"I'm not goin' to school without you," Ray said.

Ivy relaxed her shoulders, *Oh not this again*, she thought. "We've already talked about this. It's best for you to go and me to stay here and go to Rutgers so that…"

"I know what the agreement was, and I've changed my mind."

"You know my father ain't gonna have it so don't be crazy, Ray. You're going to Delaware, and I'm going to Rutgers."

"I ain't goin' nowhere without you."

"What brought this on?" Ivy was puzzled; why did Ray want to deviate from the plan that was already in motion? He had already signed the contract for a full football scholarship at Delaware State University, and she had been accepted by Rutgers University in Camden.

"You remember Cheryl and Bishop?"

Ivy stared at him. She sat down in one of the two white rocking chairs on the porch. She remembered that the couple had graduated two years earlier. Bishop went to Georgia Tech on a football scholarship, and Cheryl stayed behind and attended Camden County Community College. When Bishop came home for spring break, he found out that Cheryl was dating a guy ten years her senior. Bishop was heartbroken. He returned to school for the fall semester and, as far as everyone else knew, had moved on with his life. During the Christmas holiday, Ray found out that Bishop had dropped out of college and was now working as a construction laborer.

"Yeah, I remember Cheryl and Bishop, but Ray, you're not Bishop and I'm not Cheryl."

"Yeah. Well, you're finer than her and look what happened to them. I'm not goin' to school without you."

Ivy laughed as she stood up and put her arms around Ray's waist. "I'm not gonna let anyone take me from you."

Ray was serious. "I'm not playin', Ivy. I mean what I say."

Ivy stepped back and looked up at him. "You don't trust me?"

"Not you. I don't trust myself."

Ivy immediately thought about Ray's admission of indiscretion with a classmate of theirs. "Is Sonya Bunch goin' to Delaware?"

"No. I've been thinking about that scripture your grandfather preached on few months ago." Ivy looked at him, perplexed. "*It's better to marry than to burn.* You remember that?"

"Of course I do. You must have asked a thousand questions after he preached that sermon."

"Well, that's where I am. I'm burning up with desire for you and I'm tired of burnin'."

"I thought you took care of that itch with Sonya."

"Now, see, there you go. You said you wouldn't bring that up ever again. You said that you forgave me."

"I'm not the one who brought it up. You did," she argued.

"I beg your pardon. You brought her into this conversation, not me."

Ivy folded her arms across her chest and turned her back to Ray. No words passed for a moment and then Ivy walked off the back porch and into the yard. Ray was on her trail. She straddled the bench of the picnic table and sat down. Ray moved in front of her, straddling the bench as he sat. Placing his index finger under her chin, he gently tilted her face up so he could get eye contact.

"I love you, Ivy. I always have and I always will. You know that." He pulled her closer to him by pulling her legs on top of his. He wrapped his arms around her and began to stroke her back.

"You cheated on me, Ray. I was supposed to be the first and only one you made love to, and you cheated me out of that."

What Ivy didn't know, then, was that Sonya Bunch was not the first girl he'd been with. There were numerous others. Some of them were much older than he was. Ray let her pout as he held her. He didn't utter a word to defend himself. She was right, and he had been wrong. She was virtuous and he was sinful. He realized long ago that if Ivy had done some of the things he had, he probably wouldn't give her the time of day, and he certainly wouldn't want to marry her.

A barking dog got their attention, and the both of them realized the intimacy of their position on the bench as Ray released her. When Ivy moved away from him, he took her by the hand, not letting her go far from him.

"I'm gonna talk to the folks today during the barbeque."

"Well, you'll be pushin' a big rock up a steep hill, 'cause you know my father ain't gonna allow it."

"He don't have to allow it. We're grown people. We make our own choices. I'm not goin' to Delaware without you and that's the bottom line."

"Ray, let's just wait a year. Let's see what happens and then…"

"What's the matter? You don't wanna be with me?"

"You know that's not it."

"Then let me handle the folks. If they don't like it, then that's just too bad."

"Let's think about it."

"I've been thinkin' about it. I've been thinkin' about it since Christmas. My mind hasn't changed. It's your father and my mother that have the problem."

"What are we goin' to do? How will we live? We need money, Ray. And, what about me? I want to get a degree, too."

"I've already checked into that. You can take classes too."

"You've checked into it?"

"Yeah, and I have housing set up already. The coach said he'd put us in an apartment on campus. They're plenty of married students there."

Ivy stared at him. "You don't have to do this, Ray. I don't care about what you did in the past. You don't have to do this to prove anything to me. I promise you, as God is my witness, I'll be here waitin' for you when you come home unless death comes callin'."

"That's not why I want us to do this."

"Well, if you're worried about you leavin' me, then that only means we weren't meant to be. What God has for me is for me, and no devil in hell will keep me from gettin' it."

"You don't know the devils I know. "

She playfully punched Ray in the arm. "I'm serious."

"I'm serious, too. I want you. I want to be with you. Right now. I'm not waitin' another four years. So don't ask me to anymore.

She paused. "You really want to do this, don't you?"

"Yeah, I really want to do this. I can't leave you behind. I've got to have you with me."

"What if they say no?"

"Then we'll elope," he said with finality

The Fourth of July barbeque was wonderful that year. Both Ivy and Ray's parents' yards were used to hold all the festivities. There were horseshoes, volleyball, badminton, baseball, and rounds of UNO being played. A lot of the older people played bingo for prizes. The aboveground pool was the life of the party for the younger people. There were probably close to sixty people enjoying themselves between the two yards. It was the first time that Ivy's grandfather, who was pastor of their church, didn't attend because of illness.

Later that evening, the crowd began to thin out, moving to the waterfront near the Aquarium to see the fireworks. Ray asked to speak to both their parents in the living room of Ivy's house. After they were all seated, Ray began his speech.

"We just want everyone to know that we've changed our minds. We want to get married before I leave for Delaware."

"What are you talking about?" Ray's mother asked, almost leaping from the sofa.

"Now, wait a minute, let's not get too hysterical," Ivy's father said as he stood up from his chair, trying to calm the matter. "Ray, son, we've been through this already. We all agreed that you both need to wait until..."

"We don't want to wait anymore. Besides, you all are the ones that want us to wait."

"Oh, my God, she's pregnant." Ivy couldn't believe her mother thought such a thing.

"No! Mama, I'm not pregnant."

"Then why all of a sudden do you have to marry now?" Ivy's father asked.

"Because I love her, and I don't want to go to school without her. I don't want to be away from her. Why can't you all understand that?"

"Ray, you're only eighteen, son."

"I'm nineteen, and I know I don't want to be with anyone else but Ivy. I know I don't want to live in Delaware without her. So that you all know, I'm not leavin' here without her."

"You know, boy, you've lost your mind," Ray's mother said to him. "This girl isn't going anywhere. She'll be here waiting for you, and do you know why? Well, I'll tell you why. It's because she knows you're going be a star and make a ton of money."

Ivy and her parents were appalled and the gasp in the room was audible. Ivy's mouth hung wide open.

Ray saw the frustration and humiliation on Ivy's face. "You're wrong, Mom. Ivy's not that way at all. Neither are her parents, and you know that."

"I don't know any such thing. All I know is you and this girl have been talking about getting married since last year."

"Actually, we've been talkin' 'bout it since we were freshmen in high school."

Ray's father spoke for the first time since the conversation started. "Son, you can wait until you graduate. You need to be able to grow up completely, date other girls and…"

"I don't want to date other girls, Dad. I just want to be with her," Ray pointed at Ivy. "Look, if you all don't want to support us, then that's your business. Me and Ivy are grown, and we really don't need your permission." He looked over at Ivy. "No matter what you all say or what you think, we're gettin' married anyway."

Ray's mother was in a hiss. "Over my dead body! That girl has your nose open so wide I can see your brain, boy. And I know you're not using it at all. They'll be more tail to chase than her narrow behind."

Patricia Jones sprang from her chair and stood right in Ray's mother's face. She had had enough. "Now wait just a minute, Anna."

Ivy's father rushed over to his wife. He had to calm the situation before Anna B. Miller ended up getting decked by his wife. "Pat!" He tried pulling her away from Anna.

"Oh, no, no, no James; I'm getting ready to knock her flat on her behind! The ghetto is g'tting' ready to come out in me. I'll lay my religion down, whoop her tail, repent, and pick it back up after I dust her tail off!"

"Now, let's just calm down. Sit down, Pat. We'll work this out. No need for us to be at each other's throats."

"She looked at you and said she's not pregnant, but I just bet you she is." Ray's mother was adamant. "Why else would my son want to marry her in this stage of his life?"

"I'm not pregnant," Ivy retorted.

"If my daughter said she's not pregnant, Anna, then she's not pregnant," Pat said between clinched teeth.

"Anna, you know as well as all of us that Ray and Ivy have been infatuated with each other since the day they met," Ivy's father said, still attempting to bring calmness to the situation. "Now, I don't approve of them marrying at such a young age, however, if they want to do the right thing, then that's only because we brought them up right."

"Why are they trying to do the right thing now?" Anna questioned. "They have been doing what they please for years. Now all of a sudden, they want to act innocent. My son is not a virgin and I know it. Now tell me I'm wrong, Ray."

Ray dropped his head, sat in the wing back chair near the front door, and didn't say a word of protest. Ivy watched him retreat, knowing his mother was right, sucked her teeth, and rolled her eyes at him while thinking about Sonya Bunch.

"And if she's not pregnant, that's only because she's been lucky."

Ivy had had enough of Anna's accusations. Feeling hurt, she said, "It would have to be a miracle for conception to have happened," as a tear trickled down her left cheek. She held her head up as she pushed strength from deep inside herself. "I'm still a virgin." Then she reiterated by putting emphasis on each word. "I've never been with Ray or any other boy." She turned and dashed up the stairs.

Ivy's mother was about to say something until Ray stood to his full height of six feet, four inches. Being larger than every other man in the room, weighing more than two hundred twenty pounds, Ray shouted, "That's it!" He moved over to the stairs that Ivy used to escape the room from. "That's the last insult I'm gonna take from you today, Mom. I love her and I'm gonna marry her before I go to school; so you better get over it."

"Son, your mother just wants what's best for you," Ray's father said.

"She is what's best for me. I'm the one that's not good enough for her." Then he turned to Ivy's father. "I promise you, Mr. Jones, I'll be good to her and love her until the day I die. It's true; I'm not a saint. Ivy knows that but she loves me in spite of it." Ray looked up the stairs and then looked back at Ivy's father. "Can I go up to see about her, sir?"

Ivy's father glared up at him, not answering at first. Ray looked toward the stairs again and yelled Ivy's name from the top of his lungs.

"Go on upstairs, son. Go see about your fiancée," James finally answered.

Ray disappeared up the stairs taking them two by two.

James Jones turned his attention back to the group of people in the living room. "We all thought when they were children that this thing between them would burn itself out. Well, it didn't. They got older and the infatuation grew. And now whether we like it or not, they are in love. I know they have a rough road ahead of them. But then, so did Pat and I. And I'm sure, Carson, you and Anna have had some rough times, too. However, we're still married. If we fight them, it will only make the road more difficult for them." He looked around the room. "Now, I don't know about you all, but I want to be here for them when they need us. I'm not fighting them anymore. We are going to share grandchildren together, whether we like it or not. I'm just glad they want to do the right thing."

"You all can accept this, but I'm not." Anna stood up "I see your daughter for what she really is, and that's a gold-seeking little…"

"Get out of my house before I throw you out." The words had come out so lethal that James did a double take at his wife. Without moving from her sitting position, Pat gave the couple a direct stare. "I mean right now, get out."

Anna and Carson left without saying goodnight.

* * *

When Ray got to Ivy's bedroom, she was stretched across her bed, lying on her stomach, with her face buried in a pillow, crying her eyes out. He sat on the side of her bed and began stoking her back in an effort to comfort her. When the tears finally subsided, Ivy felt drained. Finally she sat up, sitting Indian-style with the pillow she had cried on lying across her lap.

Ray did not utter a word. He only knew he had to be there for her. He stoked the side of her face with the back of his hand.

"I know she hates me for sure now," Ivy said to Ray.

"Well, you did take her little boy from her," Ray pointed out, jokingly.

"I'm serious, Ray. Now that I know she hates me, I don't wanna be around her. And if we marry, I won't be able to avoid her. She's your mother, for goodness sake."

"She'll come around. You'll see."

"What if she doesn't? It's her blood that runs through your veins. A wife, you can divorce and get another. A mother…"

"Hush." Ray interrupted her. "I love you, girl. If my mother loves me and I know she does, she'll accept you. If she don't, then she'll lose a son instead of gaining a daughter. Now, you love me don't you?"

"With every beat of my heart," Ivy answered honestly and without hesitation.

"Then we can make it. I'm going to take care of you. I'm gonna have you livin' like the queen you are, watch and see." They smiled at each other. "Now, I have somethin' for you. Close your eyes for a second." He reached into his pockets and withdrew a small velvet box. He opened the top and said, "Give me your hand, but don't open your eyes." He slid the ring on the third finger of her left hand. "Now, open," he commanded. "I know it's not much, but it's all I could afford right now.

I promise you one day you'll have a nice, big carat on your finger."

Ivy was too astonished to speak. The stone was small but Ivy loved the ring the moment she laid eyes on it.

"It's beautiful, Ray. Thank you." She put her arms around his neck and kissed him. She released him, leaned back and looked directly into his eyes. "Now, since it's official, if I ever see you near Sonya Bunch again, I'm gonna break both your legs."

Ray tilted his head back and bellowed in laughter. "Oh, no. Not the legs, baby. I need them to make your dreams come true."

Ivy pushed her hand against his shoulder, not moving him one inch. She didn't want to joke about Sonya Bunch; she still wanted to be angry with him, but found she couldn't with such a beautiful declaration of love on her finger.

"You've got two weeks. We'll do it on a Saturday. I already asked your grandfather to perform the ceremony."

"You did?" Ivy was stunned.

"Yeah, I did. He told me to see him after I talked to his son."

Ray kissed her on the tip of her nose and moved from the bed to the door. "I better get out of here. I don't want you to lose your virtuous woman status." He started out the door.

"Raymond," Ivy called to him, stopping his retreat.

"Yeah, baby," he answered in a low soothing voice.

"I'll have everything done in less than two weeks."

He simply acknowledged her with a wink of his eye.

Chapter Twelve

Ivy could still remember everything about her wedding.

With the help of members of the church family, it had only taken ten days to put the wedding together. She and Ray visited the college just three days before they married to ensure Ivy was able to get into the classes she needed, and also to allow them to visit the campus housing.

It had been a hectic time, especially with the lack of cooperation on the part of Ray's family – it meant that the entire financial burden was on the Jones family, including all of Ray's personal needs, from his haircut to his tuxedo rental. If Ivy and Ray had had their way, they would have gone to a Justice of the Peace, or had a ceremony in Ivy's parents' living room or even the pastor's study. They knew they had not been prepared for anything elaborate, so either of those options would have been fine with them, followed by a simple reception dinner at Ivy's parent's home.

Patricia Jones, however, wanted her daughter to have a full traditional wedding including groomsmen, bridesmaids, ushers, a twelve-layer wedding cake, and a full reception with a sit-down dinner catered by one of Philadelphia's top caterers.

Needless to say, Ivy's parents spared no expense for their only daughter's wedding.

Through gossip, Anna had spread the word that she and her family would not be attending the ceremony and continued to promote Ivy as a gold digger. Just two days before the wedding, Ivy's grandfather, who was pastor at the time, visited Carson and Anna Miller at their home. No one ever knew what Pastor Jones said, during his visit. Whatever it was, though, it stopped Anna's gossiping and the family did attend the wedding.

Sheena was Ivy's maid of honor and she had hung back to wait in the choir dressing room, just outside the annex, with Ivy while the bridesmaids made their way down the aisle.

"I'm nervous, Sheena. Where's my father? He should be here. They've started already, haven't they?" Ivy was pacing the floor.

"Calm down, girl. He's standing right outside the door. And stop pacing, 'cause you're making me nervous too."

Ivy stopped. "I'm sorry." She looked toward the ceiling. "God, how did I let Ray talk me into this?"

"You know how." Sheena answered matter-of-factly. "'Cause you love him, that's how!" They shared a smile, and then Sheena turned serious. "I need to tell you something though before you go out there."

"What?"

"You're not going to believe this, but Ray's family is here!"

"Really, Sheena?" Ivy was delighted. "Thank God. That's great!"

"Yeah, they were just ushered in and are sitting on the front pew."

"Okay." Ivy frowned. "So why do you have that look on your face?"

Sheena hesitated, pressing her lips together. Finally she said, "Anna Miller is dressed completely in black."

"Well," Ivy said slowly, trying not to let it get too much to her, "she's certainly making a statement, isn't she?" But in reality she felt close to tears. It was hard to understand how the woman could be so mean.

"Forget her. God has ordained this day. If she doesn't like it, she has to take it up with the Father."

Ivy dropped her head, "I guess Granddaddy didn't fix things after all."

As if on cue, Ivy's mother entered the room and without a word walked straight up to Ivy and embraced her. Before Ivy could get any more emotional than she already was, her mother gently whispered, "Don't let the devil steal your joy. This is your day. Your father and I have spent a lot of money to make this the most special day of your life. So don't let anything or anyone spoil it for you, you hear me?" When Ivy didn't answer, Pat stepped back to look her daughter directly in the eyes.

There was still sadness in Ivy's voice. "Yes, Mama, I hear you."

"Good!" Pat headed for the door. Just as she opened it to walk out, she looked back at the girls and said, "Now, let's go kick the devil's ass." She slammed the door and was gone.

Both Sheena's and Ivy's mouths dropped.

* * *

"Girl, I remember that," Sheena stood and picked up a photo of Ivy's parents that was sitting on her nightstand. "Your mother was a loaded gun that day. And it's a good thing that's all Anna did, 'cause I think Ms. Pat would have given her an old-fashioned beat-down." The girls giggled. Sheena rested the photo back in place.

"Ray was so angry with her," Ivy remembered. "He was so mad at her that he didn't speak to her until Christmas. And that was only because the EMS rushed her to the hospital with that fake heart attack."

"Oh, it wasn't serious? Jade asked.

"No. She was released that same evening. I knew it wasn't serious. Messed up our first Christmas together. Poor Ray thought she was going to die with him not forgiving her. Had my husband tore up from the flo up!"

"Well, all I know is that everyone knew what an idiot she was, after that day. She really made a complete fool of herself," Sheena said.

"I kept thinkin' when granddaddy gets to that part that says, 'if anyone knows of any reason why these two shouldn't be joined in holy matrimony let them speak now or forever hold their peace,' Anna was gonna get up and say her piece," Miranda joked.

"Girl, I was shaking in my shoes during that whole part of the ceremony!" Ivy laughed.

Jade was sitting at Ivy's dressing-table, looking at her own reflection in the mirror, examining various lipsticks. "Let me ask you something, Ivy."

"Sure."

"Do you remember when Anna turned against you? "

Ivy thought about the question a moment. "Actually, it happened gradually. It wasn't like one day she liked me and the next day she hated the ground I walked on. But I really felt the friction in our relationship after Ray and I got home at four in the morning because Darrell's car broke down in Hershey, and Ray didn't want to call our parents for help." Ivy dropped her head. "Now that I think about it I'm under the impression she thought we were laid up someplace in a hotel or something." A few moments passed in silence. "You know, I've decided not to go to the wake."

Miranda responded first. "Ivy, you can't do that," she drawled. "If you think your name is mud now, don't show up at the wake and God only knows what you'll be then."

"Well, I'm not goin'. So, they can say what they want to say and they can call me whatever they want to call me. I don't want to go through sitting there twice and upsetting my children and myself twice. Once is enough, thank you." Ivy drew her knees up to her chest and defiantly encircled them with her arms.

Jade put down the tube of lipstick she had been examining. "Well, all I can say is, if you don't show your face at the public viewing, Anna will hang you up to dry."

Ivy pointed at her own face, still defiant. "Does it look like I care?"

"No, I don't think you do," Jade conceded.

"Look, I'm damned if I do and damned if I don't. That woman can say or do anything she pleases. I'm not taking my children through that but once. We'll do our mourning at the funeral, where it's proper, not at some wake or public viewing or whatever it is they choose to call it."

"Well, I think you really need to pray about that," Miranda twisted one of her dreadlocks.

"I have prayed about it. I never wanted a wake in the first place. But Mama said since the funeral was private, I needed to have a public viewing of some sort."

"Well, I don't know how private the funeral's going to be if Anna can invite anyone she wants," Jade remarked, going back to exploring Ivy's makeup choices.

"I'm stuck there, too. It's her son. We're having the funeral on a day she didn't want it. It's the least I can do." There was a knock on the door and Ivy raised her voice. "Come in!"

Ivy's mother stepped into the room, put her hands on her hips and scolded, "You all know you should be out here mingling with the visitors. What's wrong with you? I know you've been raised better than this."

"Give us a minute, Mama. They'll be back out there," Ivy answered.

"They? What about you, young lady?"

"I don't feel like mingling, so I'm not..."

"Ivy." Patricia's voice was flat.

"I mean it, Mama. I feel too overwhelmed to mingle right now."

Her mother looked at her sternly. "Bill is here to see you."

"What does he want now?" Ivy flopped back on her bed and stared at the ceiling.

"Did you not have that man change some of the arrangements for the funeral?"

Ivy looked at her mother for a moment before answering, "yes."

"Then you need to come out here and see him."

"I don't want to. All those people out there – they're here for the drama. I just want to be with my girls now."

"Ivy, that's not fair. Most of the people out there are members of our church. They've known you since the day you were born. I know you don't believe that Mother Evans is here for the drama of the moment."

She took a deep breath. "Well, maybe not Mother Evans, but..." She couldn't complete her sentence. Ivy thought about some of the other members of the church who had shown nothing but love toward her for as far back as she could remember. Mother Henry, who was the oldest member, had proclaimed Ivy as her granddaughter when she was five years old. Then there was Ethel Pride. She had been Ivy's babysitter when she was a child and treated her as one of her own. "I'll be out in a moment."

"Good." Her mother turned and left the room.

* * *

Once again Ivy had to endure the steady pace of visitors and hear the same phrases repeated over and over again. *I'm sorry for your loss. He'll be missed. I'm praying for you.*

Bill Hart waited until after she worked her way around the large groups of people, greeting each with a sad smile on her face.

Finally Ivy settled herself at the kitchen table with her head bowed and her hands clasped when Bill approached her. She looked up when she saw his shadow. "Oh, Bill, I'm so sorry! I forgot..."

He raised his hand to stop her words. "I understand. Don't worry about it. Can I sit down?"

"Please do."

"Our friendly funeral director was glad that you made that call. He was more than happy to make the changes. I do believe he won't have to direct another funeral for a month."

"Whew, you spent that much money?"

"Trust me, you'll be pleased."

Ivy's look held her gratitude. "Thanks, Bill. I do trust you. You have always been a good friend to Ray, and I appreciate that."

Bill reached across the table and covered her small hands with his. "I'm your friend too."

With glassy eyes, she looked directly at him and silently nodded.

Bill smiled at her and stood. "Just remember that if you need anything, and I mean anything at all, call me. Okay?"

"I will."

"You have my home number, don't you?"

"Yeah. I have Ray's phone book."

"Good. See you tomorrow."

* * *

When Bill reached his car, he dialed his best friend's number. "Hey, Marshall."

"Hey, man, what's up?"

"I'm not going to be able to handle it."

"Man, what do you mean you can't handle it? You can if you want to."

"Look, man, you know as well as I do that I've been attracted to Ivy since the day I met her. I just left her house. The woman is in bereavement and all I'm thinking about are all the things I would like to do to make her forget all about her pain."

"And that's a bad thing?"

"Why am I talking to you? You're as sick as I am."

Marshall laughed. "Look, if you still want me to take her over as a client, I will. But not charging her a fee is out of the question."

"Look, all I want you to do is meet with her whenever she needs legal advice. I'll do the legwork. You'll be getting all the credit."

"But I won't be making any money. I can't give her my time for free, Bill. I'm not you. I'm not in love with her. For me, she's dollars and cents. They're all dollars and cents."

"Then charge her the standard hourly rate for whenever you meet with her."

"You are sick, you know that?"

"I just need to keep my distance." He sighed. This was getting more complicated all the time.

"Is she still treating you cold as ice or has this whole ordeal melted her a tad?"

"We're all right. Look, on Friday I'm going to let her know you'll be handling all her legal needs, okay?"

"Whatever you say, man. But I need you to come by my office after you've read that will. I have a second part to it."

"What do you mean, a second part?"

"When Ray updated his will at your office, he came to me and added something just for you. So, see me on Friday."

Bill was stunned. "You're joking, right?"

"No, I'm not joking. I'll see you on Friday." Marshall hung up the phone.

It took a full minute for Bill to take the phone from his ear.

Chapter Thirteen

Ivy and her children did not attend the public viewing of her husband, as planned. Ray's mother, predictably, expressed her complete displeasure to everyone who would listen.

"How'd he look?" Ivy asked her friends after they entered the kitchen in search of food after the wake.

Miranda placed a potato chip in her mouth and mumbled, "He looks just like he's sleepin,' girl."

"Thompson's really did a great job. They always do. I remember when my Aunt Katherine died, they made her look the best she'd looked in years," Sheena said.

Ivy was somber. "Where's Jade?"

"She went to meet Darrell at his mother's house to check on Dee."

Ivy slumped into a chair at the table. She wove her hands together and bowed her head, "Ray Junior told me he wanted to go." She looked up and admitted, "I should have asked him if he wanted to go. He's old enough to have made that choice. I could have let him go with you all." She paused and took a deep breath, "But he didn't tell me this until about five minutes ago."

"I'm glad you didn't let him go," Sheena said.

"Why?"

"Cause a lot of the people there were ignorant as hell," Miranda answered, still picking through the potato chips.

"Randi," Sheena warned.

"Well, she needs to know what to expect tomorrow," Miranda drawled. "It's up to us to prepare her and all."

Sheena waved her hand. "Most of those people won't even be there tomorrow."

"Humph, wanna bet? All I know is the child didn't need to see all those hoochie mamas fallin' all over his Daddy's body. I know the mortician will have to clean his face and rearrange his clothes before the funeral," Miranda moved to the refrigerator and poured herself a glass of juice.

"I can't believe they were kissing on him like he could feel it," Sheena agreed. "It was disgusting."

"Oh no. That was mild compared to Ms. Thing putting a pair of her red panties in the man's coffin. You want some juice, Sheena?"

"No, thanks, but I'd love some water. Can you put some ice in it, too, please?"

Ivy was still focused on the most hurtful words. "Someone put their panties in my husband casket?"

"Downright disgraceful." Sheena dipped a cracker in cheese dip.

"Downright ignorant," Miranda added.

"No, Ivy, you did right by not going. You didn't need to be at that sideshow."

"I know that's right," Miranda confirmed.

"I guess I don't have to ask who put the panties in the coffin."

The women looked at each other. "It wasn't Caroline Hall."

There was a moment of silence in the kitchen. "I think we talk too much," Miranda said slowly.

Ivy leaned her back in her chair. "I always knew Ray had groupies. I just... he never..." She never finished the sentence as the tears took over again.

* * *

Jade met Darrell at his parents' home after she left Ray's wake. She was startled when Darrell opened the door before she could even knock. "Hey, babe."

"Hi. You surprised me!"

"I'm sorry – I didn't mean to scare you. Come on in." He took her hand and led her into the living room. "Let me help you out of your coat."

"Thanks."

"I'm still a gentlemen."

"Yes, you are," she said, smiling at him.

Darrell waved his hand toward the sitting area. "Have a seat." Jade perched on the edge of the loveseat, wondering exactly what was going on. Darrell, however, was hospitality personified. "Would you like something to drink? I have some sparkling cider I know it's one of your favorites."

"That would be nice, thanks."

"I'll be right back."

After he left Jade stood up again and explored the room. There was a framed photograph of her son with

Darrell, and another with his parents, sitting on the mantle above the fireplace. She picked up the frame that held the picture of Dee and Darrell and stroked her hand across the glass. *What have I gotten myself into?* she wondered, not for the first time.

She turned as Darrell strolled into the room with two flutes in his hands. "For you, my lady," he said, smiling, handing her the glass.

"Thanks. When did you all take these pictures?" Jade put the photograph back and sat down again, sipping her cider. It felt strange, seeing Dee's picture in someone else's house. Almost scary.

"Sunday. I think Dad took about three rolls of film!" Darrell was in a good mood about it all, anyway. "The man purchased ten photo albums, not two or three, mind you, but ten!" Darrell snickered. "I tried to tell him that was overkill, but once my mother disagreed with me then went back into the store to get even more, I knew to just close my mouth about it."

Jade smiled in spite of her misgivings. "Well I know he can be a handful, so I'm glad they're enjoying him. You aren't letting him wear them out, are you?"

"No, not at all. I had to make an appointment just to have breakfast with my own son this morning. They won't let the kid out of their sight." Jade laughed out loud and Darrell's voice became tender. "It's great to hear you laugh again."

Jade looked up at him. "Where are they now?"

"They went to the Dutch Country."

"Dutch Country?" She didn't try to hide her surprise.

"Yeah, Mom and Dad insisted that he go with them."

"He's rather young for that."

"Yeah, I know. I tried to tell them just that, but they wanted to take him anyway." He cracked a smile, "to show him off no doubt."

"Show him off?

"Yeah, a few of the church members went too."

"Ooh, I see."

They'll be back in the morning." He seemed unconcerned. "I have the room number at the hotel they're staying in if you want to call him later on tonight. Mom told me to be sure to give it to you. Let me get it. Hold on, I have the paper she wrote it on..."

"Darrell." He turned and looked at her without answering. No words passed between them, but Darrell knew she was no fool. From the way she looked at him he knew she knew he was up to something. Jade patted the seat next to her and Darrell came to sit there. "Since my son isn't here, why did you ask me to come over?"

He blew out a sigh. "Because we need to talk," he said softly.

"And it couldn't wait until after Ray's funeral?"

"No, Jade, I really need to talk to you now." He hesitated, and then went on. "I've talked to your mother. And I understand that she hadn't seen you in almost a year."

"Why did you need to talk to my mother?" Jade couldn't believe he would intrude that far into her life. She had been right to feel uneasy, before. Her nose flared and she closed her eyes to maintain her composure.

"Because there're so many unanswered questions. I'm just trying to get to the bottom of all this." He seemed to find nothing wrong with what he had done.

"Darrell."

He was off on his own track. "You didn't even tell your mother I was Dee's father! Didn't anybody question you about who his father was?"

Jade knew that anything she said would just make the situation worse. She sipped her cider instead, looking anywhere but at Darrell.

"You're not going to answer me?"

Silence.

"Jade just tell me why, why did you leave me to think that you'd had an affair and were pregnant with another man's child?"

Silence.

"Why did you lie and tell me you'd lost the baby… no, excuse me, that you were getting an abortion?"

Silence.

"Did you really think he was somebody else's child? When you left, did you really plan to have the abortion?"

Silence.

"Jade, please, I have to know."

She raised her head and looked directly at him. "You can save you breath, Darrell, because I'm not telling you. What happened has happened, and there's nothing that can change that. I've apologized to you and I'm not going to continue apologizing for the rest of my life. It was done and that's that."

Darrell felt stunned. Why was she refusing him the answers he deserved? Why was she so angry? He took both her hands in his. "Okay. Okay, baby. That's not what's really important right now. Let's look at the future."

Jade pulled her hands away and folded them across her lap. "Now that, I can talk about."

"Well, that's another reason why I wanted to talk to your parents and mine. Together."

Jade raised her eyebrows.

"I had your parents here for dinner on Sunday. Your sister came too." Darrell smiled in spite of his concern, remembering her younger sister and how beautiful she was becoming. "She's really growing up. She looks just like you."

Jade was not amused. "Get to the point, Darrell."

"We… I mean… we talked about it… and well, all of us think that the best thing for us to do is to get married."

Jade's eyes widened in surprise. *Oh, no he didn't just say what he and everyone else thinks I should do,* she thought.

"I know you have a good job in Maryland," Darrell continued, "but I'm working for a great engineering firm here in Philly. I can support us. And if you feel like you want to continue working outside the home, you can do that, too. You can even go back and finish law school. Your mother mentioned that going back to school was something you really want to do. And my mother said she don't mind babysitting."

Jade was astonished. *With all that has happened between us he wants to marry me*, she thought as she shook her head in disbelief.

"Don't just say no, Jade," he said. "We need to think this thing through. You want to be with *our* son." Jade rolled her eyes to the ceiling. "I want to be with *our* son. And the only way to be with him at the same time is for us to be living under the same roof."

Jade said, as calmly as possible, "You know as well as I do that we don't have to be under the same roof to share *our* son, Darrell. There are thousands of kids out there with parents who live apart."

"Is that really what you want for our son, Jade?"

"Darrell, we are no longer together. I live alone. I don't even date. I don't want a relationship with anyone. I just want to live my life as quietly as possible with nothing other than *our* son to answer for. You don't need me in your life to be with your son."

"Don't tell me what I do and do not need."

"Why not? That's exactly what you just did to me!" Jade stood abruptly and walked over to the mantle where her son's pictures sat. She picked up a frame and said, "I know how you feel about family and I'm sure being with Dee these last few days has had you thinking that maybe we could be a family," she replaced the photo back on the mantle, "when in fact we will never be a family. I don't want a family. I'm not cut out for marriage. I think the best thing for you to do is to find you a wonderful saved woman who will be able to give you what you're looking for."

"I don't want a wonderful saved woman, I want…"

"As for Dee, I'll bring him here every weekend if that's what you want. I'm willing to work with you with any kind of arrangements you want. I'll even drive him here myself on weekends. And when he's old enough he can take the train from Baltimore to 30th Street Station. I just don't want any parts of marriage or being with any man." She took a deep breath. "Period."

Darrell got up and came to stand next to her. "What happened, Jade? Who turned you against the whole institution of marriage?"

"Marriage is fine for you and a billion other people in the world. Okay? It's just not for me!" The young street-smart Jade was coming out again. "It's none of your business, frankly, how I feel or why I feel the way I do. Can I have my coat, now, please?"

"Why do you need your coat? We're not finished yet."

"Oh yes, we are. There's nothing more for me to say." Jade walked past him and stood at the front door. Darrell followed her. "My coat, please."

"I'm not finished talking to you, Jade."

"I'm finished. All you have to do is let me know what type of arrangements you'd like to make to see Dee and I promise I'll do my best to arrange my schedule to get him here." Jade said with finality. "Now, please give me my coat."

"I can tell you now what I want."

"Okay, tell me," she said as she folded her arms across her chest.

"I want to see him every day of his life until he's twenty-one years old. I want him in the same city I live in and I want to be able to see him anytime I want, day or night." He stepped closer to her. "So if I want to sit by his bedside and stare at him while he's sleeping I can, or if I want to be there to make pancakes with the chocolate chips in them for him in the morning, I can."

Jade looked at him as if he'd lost his mind. "Now that's just ridiculous."

"You think so."

"I'm not going to argue with you. You told me we weren't going to fight."

"I'm not fighting with you. I want what I want."

"What you want isn't reasonable."

"But your not giving me an opinion at all was reasonable?"

Jade strode back into the living room to get her purse. "Can I have my coat please?"

"We're not finished."

"Yes. We are. I don't have anything else to say to you." Jade remembered what Sheena had told her and she repeated part of it to Darrell. "If you want a fight, then I'll give you the fight of your life. So I guess you and I will see each other in court." She started for the door again. Darrell rushed to the door and stood in front of it. "Move, Darrell, I'm leaving."

"Jade, wait."

"No, get out of my way." She was fuming.

"Don't you want your coat?"

"No, you keep it." Jade reached for the door handle. "Let your parents know I'll be here tomorrow for my son." She was prepared to leave without her coat.

"Jade." He rubbed his hand down her arm in an attempt to calm her. "I'm sorry, I didn't mean to make you angry. I just want to be with him just like you do. He's a part of me as much as he is a part of you and you're not being fair to me."

She lifted her head to look at him. "We're not really fighting about you being with Dee, are we, Darrell?"

"Not totally, no." Darrell pulled her to his chest and embraced her in his arms. "Marry me, Jade. I won't put any demands on you. If you want separate bedrooms I'm willing to do that and any other compromises you want. I just want to be under the same roof with you and *our* son."

Using the palm of her hands Jade pushed him away and wiped away the unexpected tears that were in her eyes. "You just don't get it, do you?"

"Get what?"

"I can't marry you. I know what you want, Darrell. Aren't you in seminary training?"

"What does that have to do with anything?"

"I'm not minister's wife material and I refuse to pretend I'm something that I'm not anymore."

"What are you talking about?"

"I'm leaving."

"Wait." He stood directly in front of her. "That's why all this started in the first place isn't it?" He stepped even closer to her. "It's because I told you I was going into the ministry." Jade took a step back. "Ever since I told you that I was called to preach and that we couldn't be together anymore intimately unless we were married you started acting funny."

"Please, Darrell, please move."

"You knew you were already pregnant didn't you?"

Silence

"Jade."

"Yes, I knew," was hissed between clinched teeth. "Take your hands off me. Now, let me go. Please!"

Darrell searched her eyes before he moved away from the door.

She left without a backward look and without her coat.

* * *

Ivy still had no appetite. When she was given a plate of food she attempted to eat but couldn't. Once again, her house was filled with people and she wanted to be alone. She moved around the rooms like a ghost, trying her best to be polite and hold general conversation with her visitors. More gossip about the wake found its way to Ivy's ears. From what her friends had told her, she didn't think it could get any worse.

She was wrong.

Ivy's brother John came to her that night with news of another twist of events.

She was sitting listlessly in an armchair in the small sitting area off her bedroom. "Okay, John, what is it you need to tell me?"

"I don't even know how to tell you this," John said honestly.

"Just say it, 'cause whatever it is can't be more disgusting than what I've already heard."

"I think I know why Ray wanted you to divorce him."

She didn't say anything, and the silence stretched out unbearably between them. Then John cleared his throat. "I found out last night that Caroline, well, she's pregnant, Ivy. That's why Ray's parents have included her…"

That got her attention. "This woman is pregnant and they immediately think that it's Ray's child?"

"Yeah."

Ivy began laughing, uncontrollably. Between fits of laughter she said, "This is too rich. I can't believe that wench is going to try and put a child off on my dead husband."

"Ivy it's true. She's pregnant."

"Well, I guess congratulations are in order." Her brother was about to say something when she added, with finality, "And I don't want to talk about it anymore until after Ray's burial, understood?"

"Okay."

"Please close the door behind you 'cause I'd like to be alone."

When John left the room, Ivy lifted the phone receiver that sat on her nightstand near her bed. After pressing several numbers she spoke, "Hi, Bill, this is Ivy." A pause. "You told me to call you if I needed anything, well, I need you. My brother John just told me a wild rumor, and I believe it needs to be taken care of."

Chapter Fourteen

In the brisk March wind, Bill Hart stood outside the church waiting for the family car that held Ray's widow and children to arrive. It was last evening that he had realized just how virtuous she truly was. Any other woman would have crumbled under the pressure. Yet Ivy continued to stand with integrity against all adversity. *Maybe that's why I admire her so much*, he thought. *Anna is giving her hell and Ivy takes it all in stride.*

Last night she had instructed him to send, not only one, but three oversized limousines to accommodate Anna's family for the funeral. Ray's parents had arrived just moments ago.

Just before she walked into the church, Anna told Bill she needed to talk to him about Caroline. He was still in disbelief as to how Anna could stand by her son's mistress and totally disregard his widow. Bill raised his head to attention as he saw the limousine pull to the front door of the church. As he walked toward the side door, the rear window began to come down.

"Hi, Bill," Sheena greeted him.

"Hi," he said as he bent his body to look into the car. He saw the four children, Jade, Miranda, and Ivy.

"Hey, Bill."

"Ivy."

"Have they closed the coffin yet?"

"They were about to do that when I came out here to greet you. I'll go back in now to be sure. Just wait right here."

Ivy had instructed Bill to have the coffin closed when she and the children came in. She felt that the eulogy would go much smoother if no one could see Ray. She told him that she had heard about the wake, and she did not want that same scenario played out in front of her children. Bill agreed and called the funeral home immediately to instruct them of the change. When Bill peeped into the church, ushers were fanning Anna and the coffin was just being closed.

Ivy's father, along with her mother, approached Bill. "I assume they've arrived."

"Yes sir, they just pulled up. She wanted me to be sure that everything was set for them to come in."

"It's okay. Let's go on and get this over with," Reverend Jones said as he headed out and opened the rear door of the car. "Are you ready, sweetheart?"

"As ready as I'm going to be, Daddy."

"Granddaddy, Mommy said that my Daddy won't be able to wake up and that he's in heaven living with God now," his six-year-old grandson said.

"Yes, son, that's right. And you and I will talk about that later. I promise. Granddaddy will explain everything and answer all your questions. All right?"

"Okay."

"Miranda, you stay with the girls. Jade, you take the boys. Sheena, you stick with Ivy just like we said, all right?"

"Yes, Pastor," they said, almost in unison.

Ivy sat on the right side of the church in the first pew along with her children, mother, brother, Jade, Miranda, and Sheena. Ivy's father delivered the eulogy.

During one point in the sermon, Sheena could feel Ivy trembling. She leaned over to ask if she was all right.

Ivy leaned over to her friend and whispered, "When they open the coffin and I go up there, I want you to go with me. Don't leave me there, okay?"

"Okay. I'm not gonna leave you."

The service so far had been held in decency and order. Now that they were about to open the coffin for the final viewing, Ivy was nervous. She felt as if her chest had tightened irrevocably, and she was shaking uncontrollably.

The church was silent as the funeral director began to prepare to open the casket so Ray could be viewed for the final time. When they stepped back, Ivy could see him now. Her eyes filled with tears.

"You ready to go up?" Sheena whispered to her.

Ivy nodded her head. "Bring my children. I want us to do it all together." Then she stood and looked at Ray's profile. Ray, Junior, came to stand next to his mother. He took her hand and walked toward the casket.

The closer Ivy got to Ray, the harder it was for her to breath. Her attempt to control her trembling failed, and from a distance Bill could see her swaying.

One of the twins called to her father, "Daddy. Daddy," as if she was calling to wake him from his sleep. You could hear the sniffles in the church getting louder. Ivy's son Solomon asked, "Mommy, why Daddy laying there like that?" Ivy looked over at her youngest son, who was in Jade's arms. When her baby's eyes met hers, he said, "Make Daddy get up, Mommy. Make him get up. Come on, Daddy. Let's go home. I want to go home."

The words traveled through the church and touched the hearts of the people in the sanctuary. Again, you could hear the whimpering of the congregation getting louder. Ivy opened her mouth to answer her son but each time she opened her mouth, no words would form.

"Come on Ivy. Let's sit down," Sheena told her as she felt Ivy's quivering becoming more violent.

Ignoring Sheena, Ivy put her hand on Ray's and cried out his name, as everything around her faded to black.

* * *

Bill began to work his way to the front of the church as soon as he saw Ivy begin to sway. And before her body hit the floor, Bill caught her and gathered her up in his arms.

"Let's get her to the annex. The ushers have some smelling salts back there," Sheena said to him.

The children were in a panic. Seeing Ivy pass out had frightened them. Ivy's mother came to try and help settle the children down. Ivy's father stood at the pulpit and told the ushers to help get the children to the annex. At this point, the whole church was in an uproar.

Bill never stopped with Ivy in the annex. He carried her out the front door and into the waiting limousine. He slid in the car and settled Ivy on his lap.

Ivy was totally out.

Sheena stepped into the car soon after Bill. "I have some smelling salts."

"No, don't. Let her wake up on her own."

"Bill, I don't want the kids to get in the car and see her out like a light."

Bill didn't say a word. He continued to look down at Ivy. Sheena watched him watching her. He caressed her face with his hand as he watched her.

"Bill," Sheena said urgently.

He didn't answer.

"Bill."

He looked up at Sheena, "I'm going to get my car so I can take her home."

"No, Bill. She needs to be with her children."

"Then get the kids, 'cause I'm taking her home," he said raising his voice.

Sheena was stunned. *He actually raised his voice at me*, she said to herself. She observed the concerned look on his face and the way he continued to stroke Ivy's hair. Tilting her head to one side, a thought occurred to her as she watched him. "Well, I'll be damned," Sheena said in a soft whisper. Bill looked up at her. "And she thought you didn't like her."

The car door swung open. "My mom all right?" Ray Junior asked.

"She's fine, son. She just fainted," Bill answered.

Ivy began to stir. Ray Junior was on his knees with his hand resting on his mother's belly. "Mom."

Ivy heard her son. "I'm coming," she said, disoriented, attempting to get up.

"Shhh. Be still, Ivy." Sheena's voice was gentle. "Give yourself time to recover."

"My babies! Where are my babies?" Ivy was trying to focus her eyes.

"Tamara and Terra are coming now. Open the door, Junior."

Ivy sat up. Looking at Bill she asked already knowing the answer, "I passed out?"

"Yeah," he answered. "You're okay now."

"But Bill caught you. You never hit the floor," Sheena added.

Miranda and an usher helped Ivy's girls into the car. Both girls clung to their mother, still crying. "Where's Solomon?" Ivy asked.

"Randi has him. She was right behind me. Here she is."

Ivy held her children tightly to her. "Poor things. I'm sorry I scared you," she said, over and over. "Mommy's all right. She didn't mean to scare you." She met Sheena's eyes. "I'm not going to the cemetery, Sheen," she said. "I can't handle it."

"I want to go, Mommy," Ray Junior said, immediately. "I want to see Daddy buried."

"Are you sure, baby?"

"Yes, I want to go."

"I'll go with him," Bill volunteered.

"Thank you, Bill. I'd really appreciate that."

* * *

By the time the car pulled up to Ivy's house, the children had settled down. The twins had fallen asleep, and Solomon was in dry heaves.

Miranda and Jade settled the children in their rooms, and Sheena sat next to Ivy.

"Want something to eat?"

Ivy shook her head.

"You really need to eat something. You haven't had a bite to eat since yesterday."

Silence.

Jade and Miranda entered the room. "The kids are all asleep. Even Solomon dropped off before I left him," Jade said.

Silence.

"Well," Sheena said as she stood, "I guess we need to expect that some people will be coming here in a hour or so."

"No, they're going back to the church. That's where the food will be," Miranda answered. "Ivy, you need to eat something."

"She's told everyone that she's pregnant with Ray's child." Ivy's voice was cold.

"What? Who?"

"Caroline?"

"Yeah. And she has Ray's family thinking that she's pregnant with his child." The girls were now the ones silent. "I talked to Bill last night. He's going to handle everything on Friday at the reading of the will."

"Ray, Ray, Ray, what happened, man?" Jade said to the ceiling.

Sheena sniffed. "Who told you?"

"John told me yesterday."

"I wonder if Ray knew?" Jade asked.

"No, there's no way he could have known."

"Well, don't worry about it now. Let Bill do his job. He'll take care of you," Sheena assured Ivy.

"Bill won't be doing anything for me after Friday."

"What?"

"He told me last night that he has a friend who's going to take over all my legal affairs."

Sheena stared at her in surprise. After what she had seen in the limo, this was the last thing she expected. "Did he tell you why he was doing this?"

"No, but I can guess why. Bill never really liked me. I don't know why, but he's always avoided me like the plague."

"You still want me to go with you on Friday?" Sheena asked.

"Please. You're the only one in the room with a law degree."

* * *

Ivy's parents arrived with her son and Bill a few hours later. Ivy was grateful to her mother for making sure the house didn't fill with people yet again. She just wasn't up to mingling today. She was weak. It took her mother to convince her to eat something.

Sheena managed to speak to Bill alone. "I understand you're pushing Ivy off on one of your friends."

"I'm not pushing Ivy off on anyone. Marshall's going to take good care of her. He's the best when it comes to estate law."

"Marshall? You mean Vincent Marshall?"

"Yeah, that Marshall." He frowned. "You have a problem with him?"

"He's bad, all right. But why are you really dropping her?"

"Because I want what's best for her," he answered.

"I think *you're* what's best for her. You know her, Bill. And from what I observed in the car, you genuinely care about her."

"I genuinely care about all my clients."

Sheena wasn't having any of it. "Don't screw with me, Bill. Now I understand why she thinks you hate her."

"She told you that?" He couldn't hide the surprise from his voice.

Sheena nodded her head. "Just today she said – let's see, how did she say it? Oh yeah. She said, and I quote, he avoids me like a plague."

"It's not like that."

"Really? Then how is it? You really never had anything to do with her until Ray died."

"That's because I worked for Ray, not his wife. Come on, Sheena, you know how it goes."

She stood up, unable to contain herself any longer. "I know what I saw in the limo."

"Oh, and what did you see?" He sounded defensive, which was what she had been hoping for. "You saw me being concerned about a client's widow. That's what you saw."

Sheena smiled. "You and I both are trained to interpret body language and to read minds. My intuition never leads me wrong. It's second-guessing that defeats me."

"She's going through enough. So don't go starting rumors, all right?" Sheena didn't say anything, and Bill sighed. "If you're done, I think I'll go back into the house." He turned to walk away.

"I remembered the day I introduced you," Sheena said.

Bill stopped walking and turned in Sheena's direction. "And?"

"You wanted her, Bill."

"Then I found out she was married, Sheena."

"So are you saying your feelings for her simply disappeared?"

Bill moved closer to Sheena and said, "You've always been opinionated. But you need to learn how to keep some thoughts to yourself."

Sheena raised her head with confidence and looked into his eyes. "I think you've known me long enough to know that being opinionated is part of my nature and one of the main reasons you hired me as your clerk in the first place, even though I hadn't even finished law school, Mr. Hart," she said firmly. "Let me refresh your memory."

* * *

Sheena had been hired to clerk for Bill during her last semester of college. Her employment continued during the summer as she prepared to take the bar exam. Working for Bill afforded her some experience and allowed her the use of his extensive law library to study for the test.

When Bill interviewed Sheena for the position, his first inclination was not to hire her, thinking that her mere presence would cause a distraction in his office. But after the interview, he knew that even though she was extraordinarily beautiful, she was serious about her career and could definitely handle herself. She was opinionated and a sharp thinker. Just the type of personality his office needed at that time.

Ivy was with Sheena at an upscale restaurant called Silver Lake the first time he saw her. Both he and Marshall noticed the women as they were being seated at a nearby table.

"Whew, she's drop-dead gorgeous," Marshall exclaimed.

"I'm looking at the one with the hair down her back. Which one are you looking at?" Bill asked his friend for clarification.

"I'm looking at the other one. I hate women who accessorize with fake weave. And looky, looky, baby got back. She's phat!"

"She works in my office. Her name is Sheena. She's the student I hired. She just passed the bar with a perfect score. I'm about to lose her."

"That exquisite creature is in our profession?"

"She's the one that wrote the answer for the Smith Case."

"Damn, and she's smart too. Introduce me to her," Marshall begged. Two more women approached the table and they watched as they hugged. "Whew!" Marshall exclaimed. "It's a whole craft full of fine women over there. I guess it's true, all the fine women flock together. Come on."

When they approached the table, Sheena was the one who stood. "Mr. Hart, how are you this evening?"

"I'm fine. We're not in the office, so why don't you call me Bill?"

Sheena smiled. "Everyone, this is my boss, William Hart the Third, who wants to be called Bill. Bill, these are my very close and dear friends, Miranda and Ivy, and this special woman is my mother, Christina."

"Pleased to meet you all. This is my friend, Vincent Marshall."

"Come and join us, 'cause if you don't, you may not get a table for at least another hour or so," Christina offered.

"Thank you. I'd like that very much," Bill accepted with gratitude. Marshall pulled out a chair and sat next to Sheena, while Bill sat next to Ivy.

Marshall couldn't keep his eyes off Sheena, and he was totally open about his interest in her. Bill, on the other hand, was more subtle to his approach to Ivy. So much so, in fact, that everyone at the table was clueless to his attraction to her. That is everyone except Christina. She noticed that Bill was drawn to Ivy like a moth to a flame.

When the check came, Marshall paid it and instructed Bill to take care of the gratuity. Christina excused herself, kissed each woman goodbye, and warned them not to be late for Sunday school the following morning. Sheena walked her mother to her car.

"Sunday school?" Marshall questioned.

"Yes, Sunday school. You have a problem with that?" Ivy asked.

"No, it's just that I haven't been since I was a child," he clarified.

"Well, we grew up in church. Our fathers are in the ministry."

"Ivy's father is our pastor," Miranda said.

That's what it is, Bill thought. *Oh yeah, just the kind of woman to take home for Mama to meet. The kind you marry.* "So what church do you belong to?"

"Cathedral of Faith," Ivy answered.

"Cathedral, Cathedral, oh you mean in Camden? Isn't that Ray Miller's church?" Marshall asked.

The women giggled. "Ray Miller does not own the church," Ivy said.

"No, he doesn't. I don't care how much money he makes. The church was there long before he became a member," Miranda added.

"Well, that's what I meant, the church he belongs to," Marshall corrected himself.

"Think you could introduce me to him?"

"Well, I don't know. That depends," she answered.

"Depends on what?"

"Why you want to meet him," she answered.

"I'd like to get his autograph," Marshall answered.

"No. No can do," Ivy said jokingly.

"I'll tell you what," Miranda said to Marshall. "Ivy and Ray just opened the Ray Miller Center, and the Ivy League needs donations. If you get some of your rich attorney friends to donate to the center, I'll get you more than an autograph."

"More than an autograph? You know him like that?" Marshall asked as Sheena rejoined them at the table.

"Yeah, I know him like he's a part of my family," Miranda said.

"What are we talking about?" Sheena asked.

"Donations for the Center," Miranda answered.

It was Bill's turn to intervene. "You never told me you knew Ray Miller, Sheena. I'd be interested in representing him."

"I didn't know you did entertainment or sports law," Sheena said.

"A contract with Ray Miller could get me started," Bill answered.

Sheena turned to Ivy. "When will Ray be back in town?"

"Monday," Ivy answered.

"You did tell me you were looking for a good attorney, right?" Ivy nodded. "And I'm sure since he has no experience in sports, he'll cut you a great deal to represent your husband, Ivy."

"Husband!" Marshall exclaimed.

"Yes. Ivy is Ray's wife." Marshall looked over at Bill and could see the disappointment etched on his friend's face.

* * *

Bill laughed lightly. "Was I that obvious?"

"I don't think any of us had a clue," Sheena confessed. "It was hindsight, really. That and seeing you with her today."

"What about Ivy – you're saying she never knew I was attracted to her?"

"Not a clue. Ivy was at a loss 'cause she always had eyes for Ray, and only Ray." She giggled suddenly. "Come to think of it, though, when I walked my mother to the car, she told me to be sure to let you know that Ivy was married!"

"I'm embarrassed," Bill admitted.

"Don't be," she murmured. "It was a long time ago."

"I've never disrespected them, Sheena. Never."

"I know you haven't. And I'm sure you can continue to handle her with that same integrity. She doesn't need to switch horses in the middle of the street, Bill. She needs as much stability as she can get right now. Don't make her life any harder than it already is, okay?" Sheena placed a hand on Bill's suit jacket and smoothed out his lapel. "You can always release her six months or a year from now, after she's weathered this storm. If you truly care anything for her, you'll wait."

"I'll think about it," he finally said after a brief pause.

"I know you," she said. "You'll do the right thing."

* * *

After paying his respects to Ivy, Darrell eagerly sought out Jade, finally catching up with her in the kitchen. He stood and watched for a moment as she worked her way around the stove. *Why would she think she's not marriage material?* He imagined her working her way around in their own kitchen, being hostess to one of the many social functions he knew would soon be part of his life.

She had called his parents' home early that morning, looking for their son. He convinced her to allow Dee to stay another day, since she would be tied up with Ivy and the funeral. She'd reluctantly agreed.

"Hey, Darrell!" At Pastor Jones' voice, Jade swung around to see Darrell standing near the kitchen doorway. Ivy's father shook Darrell's hand. "I haven't seen you around lately. How's everything going?"

"Everything is coming along fine, Pastor. My plate is full right now."

The Reverend Jones nodded. "I know you've been busy. I've been keeping my eye on you. I understand you're doing quite well in school."

"I'm doing all right, sir."

"Ah, now, don't be so modest. I know you're doing more than just all right. But I understand if you don't want to toot your own horn." Pastor Jones patted the younger man's shoulder and then turned to Jade. "Ah, Jade. Ivy'd like you to put this plate in the oven for her. She'll eat it later."

Jade took the plate from his outstretched hand. She was dismayed. "She's still not eating?"

"Afraid not. But that's to be expected, so don't you worry about it, all right?

"Okay, Pastor, if you say so."

Pastor Jones headed out of the kitchen, stopped abruptly and said, "If you two need some guidance, my door is always open to you." He turned to face them. "Understand?"

"Yes, sir. Understood."

"Jade?" He waited for her reply.

"Yes, Pastor, I understand."

"Good, you have to make all stumbling blocks into stepping stones," he proclaimed as he finally left the room.

Darrell leaned on the counter.

Jade kept polishing the stovetop. "How's my baby doing?"

"He's fine, Jade, just like he was this morning when you called."

"He hasn't asked for me?"

"Yeah, he has, and he's even been fretting a little. Then Mom or Dad gets him occupied with something else. But he'll be fine until tomorrow morning. I promise to bring him here bright and early."

Sheena and Miranda walked into the kitchen, chatting about something Jade couldn't hear and wasn't listening to. She walked toward the French doors and stood there a moment.

Sheena looked from Darrell to Jade. "Everything all right in here?"

"Everything's fine," Darrell said, nodding.

Jade walked through the doors into the sunroom, closing the door firmly behind her.

Sheena and Miranda watched her go and looked at each other, raising their eyebrows. Sheena turned to Darrell. "I hope you're not here to start anything," she said quietly. "It's not the time or the place."

"I've been a complete gentleman, scout's honor." He raised two fingers in an imitation of the scout's pledge; but it was Jade he was looking at, not Sheena. He cleared his throat and looked at the two women standing near him. "What happened to her? Why is she so... so... guarded?"

Sheena shrugged. "I have no idea."

Miranda shook her head. "She hasn't told us anything, Darrell."

He sighed. "Well, I did figure out that my entering the ministry has a lot to do with it. But she believes in God as much as all of us do! I can't understand why it's such a big deal."

"She's the one you'll have to get that answer from. But now is not the time," Sheena repeated, dropping her voice as Jade came back into the kitchen.

Jade walked up to the counter, looked straight at Darrell and said steadily, "I want to go get my son right now."

He was perplexed. "Jade, we talked about this. I'll bring him to you in the morning."

"No, I want him now."

Miranda glanced at Sheena and said, gently, "Jade, be reasonable. Darrell will…"

"Now!"

Sheena walked over to Jade and took her by the arm. "Stop now," she said. "What's wrong with you? Ivy doesn't need any more drama than she's already dealing with. So just chill out, Jade. The man said he'd bring Dee in the morning. If he doesn't, we'll call the police, okay? But this isn't about you, here."

"I'm not trying to take him, Jade," Darrell reassured them again.

Jade felt the wind leave her lungs. "It's not that. I… I miss him," she stuttered. "I just want to see him, that's all."

Darrell turned to Jade, took her hands, and closed his own around them. To his surprise, she didn't try to pull away. "Your biggest concern is your friend in there." He nodded his head toward the family room where Ivy was sitting. "She won't eat and probably hasn't slept in days. Our son is being cared for – and very well, with family. So you've got to forget about yourself right now and concentrate on Ivy."

"He's right, Jade," Miranda agreed.

"You'll have him here early?" She was giving in.

"Before nine, so the police won't have to be dispatched to my parents' home." He winked at Sheena and Miranda, who both giggled out loud. Jade rolled her eyes at them.

Where would he go? There is no way a minister-in-waiting would take her child. No, their child. Dee was their baby. Jade looked around the room. "Let me see if Ivy needs anything."

Chapter Fifteen

"Good morning," Miranda said the next day, wandering yawning into the kitchen. Jade was there, still in her robe, drinking coffee. Sheena was already dressed.

"Morning," they answered in unison.

"Is Ivy still asleep?"

"Yeah, thank God. I think she cried half the night," Miranda answered. "Any more coffee in that pot?"

"Well, she needed to get it all out. That's why we were right not to bother her," Sheena said.

"You're looking good. Where you going?" Miranda asked.

"To work – before I get fired," Sheena answered.

"Yeah right. Like Jason Jackson is going to let that happen," Jade said.

Sheena turned to Jade with both hands on her hips and answered, "Contrary to popular belief, Jason has a boss, too, you know."

Jade was about to retort when Miranda warned, "Jade."

"Sorry."

Turning to Sheena, Miranda asked, "Can I get a ride with you to the high speed line?"

Sheena stared at Jade as she picked up her purse. "Sure, I'll meet you in the car," she answered as she walked out of the kitchen.

Miranda turned her attention back to Jade. "Why do you like to vex her so? It's like you're playing with her head all the time."

"I don't mean to try and vex her. She's just sensitive when it comes to Jason." Perhaps realizing that she had little room to criticize, she changed the subject quickly. "Why do you need a ride to the speed line?"

"I have to be back at work today, too."

"They wouldn't allow you to take off a few extra days?"

"Girl, I dare not ask," she said as she picked up a slice of bacon from the plate sitting on the table. "They're more than generous with me already. Every time I have to take off for Momma, whether it's a treatment or she's in the hospital or whatever, they allow me to take the time I need. Believe me, the three days they gave me is more than enough.

"I noticed your mom didn't make it to the funeral. How is she feeling?"

"To be honest, I can never tell how she's feeling. She doesn't complain, not ever.

When are you leaving?" Miranda asked, sticking another piece of bacon into her mouth.

"Sunday." They both turned when they heard a car horn.

"That would be Sheena." Miranda began walking to the front door with Jade following behind her. "Oh look, Darrell's here."

Darrell was walking towards the front door with Dee in his arms. Sheena got out of her car to greet them both. "He's so cute," Jade heard Sheena say. "I'll have to take a closer look when I get back. Come on, Randi, put a move on it, please."

"I'm coming, I'm coming. So hold your horses."

Jade stood on the top landing and watched as her friends kissed and fussed over her son. "Wave bye-bye to Aunty Sheena and Aunty Miranda!" Dee waved his little arm vigorously.

After they drove away, Darrell approached the front steps where Jade was still standing on the landing. When Dee saw his mother, his eyes widened and he kicked his feet as he stretched out his arms toward her.

Jade raced down the steps to embrace her baby. "Hello, my darling. Mommy missed you so much," she said as she covered his face with kisses. Hugging the baby to her chest, she turned up the stairs to enter the house.

"Jade," Darrell called. Jade turned to look at him. "I have to be at work by nine. But we still need to talk. You know that, right?"

"Darrell, it may be best to get our attorneys involved."

"I don't want outsiders involved in our affairs. We can handle this on our own." Darrell walked up the steps and stood on the landing next to Jade. "I think we can be fair and reasonable to each other for the sake of *our* son.

"Yes, I'm sure you're right. But right now Ivy's going through a rough time. I'm here to support her and not talk about my... about our personal dilemma. When I get back home, we can handle our situation. I can't handle it until then."

Without saying a word, Darrell started for his car. Jade watched as he got in, started the engine, and drove away.

* * *

Jade was sitting in the family room with the television on when Ivy finally emerged from her room.

"Well, I see Darrell was a man of his word."

Jade looked up from the floor where she was playing with Dee. "Hey girl, get enough rest?"

"Too much rest. Why didn't you wake me?" Ivy ran her fingers through her hair.

"Because you needed the rest."

"You're probably right." She flopped down onto the sofa. "Where are my children?"

"Your parents have the boys, and Lisa has the twins."

Ivy reached down to pick up the baby. "Hey, little man," she cooed to the child as she kissed his soft cheek. "I am so hungry," she said. "Let's go get something to eat."

Getting up from the floor, Jade said, "I'll make you a big breakfast."

"No, I want to go out. IHop."

"You sure?"

"Positive."

The doorbell rang and Ivy flinched. "Who can that be now? This early?"

"Girl, it's not early. It's almost noon," Jade said as she went to answer the door.

Ivy sat the baby on the sofa and was tickling his feet when Jade came back and announced, "It's your mother-in-law."

Ivy stopped moving instantly. She closed her eyes tightly and muttered something unintelligible under her breath.

"Do you want to see her right now?"

"Yeah, I'll see her," Ivy answered. *Better get it over with.*

Ivy stood up and straightened her clothing to greet Anna Miller, entering the living-room soundlessly. Ivy cleared her throat. Anna looked up as she placed the heavy frame she had been examining back down on the table.

"Mrs. Miller."

"Ivy."

"To what do I owe the pleasure of your appearance?"

Anna stared at Ivy for a moment. As she removed her gloves from her manicured hands, she said, "I'd like to discuss a few things before we go to the reading of my son's will tomorrow."

Oh, here we go. And she says I'm the one greedy for money! "Oh, I thought maybe you wanted to know how his children are getting along."

"I know that your family will be sure that *your children* are well provided for. And now since the Jones family has taken another one of my children…"

No, she didn't just go there. Ivy couldn't let her go on. "Oh, do you mean Lisa? I understand that my brother is very much in love with her. Wonder what it is about the Millers that's so enticing to the Joneses?"

Anna stared at her. "Don't be brash with me, girl."

Don't let the devil steal your joy, Ivy told herself. "What is it that you want, Mrs. Miller?" Ivy asked, emphasizing her name.

Anna held her head high as she walked over to the bay window and looked out. "I want to be sure that all of Ray's children are taken care of."

The nerve of this wench. She has the unmitigating gall to come to my home and talk to me about Ray's bastard child? What is wrong with this woman?

"...And I think that all of Ray's children should have equal opportunity to their father's legacy. Fair is fair. The child had nothing to do with this mess you and Ray created."

Ray and I created? "No, no, Mrs. Miller. The only thing that I tried to create was a loving home for my family. Ray was my husband, not my boyfriend or a fling, I wasn't his mistress or his chick on the side." Ivy stepped closer to the bay window where Anna was standing. "I was his wife," Ivy emphasized each word. "But you know what? Above all things, I'm a holy woman of God. I will not be lowered to your standards."

"How dare you, you little..."

"I dare because you opened the door with the space and the opportunity," Ivy said raising her voice a notch.

"I came here in a civil manner and you..."

"See, now that's where we differ in opinions. I think you shouldn't have come here at all."

"This is my son's house."

"No, the mortgage company says it's my house." Anna stared at Ivy as if she didn't know what to say next. "You see, Mrs. Miller, last night I was lying there crying in my bed. And, the Lord just started speaking to me. He told me to dry my tears and be of good courage because where I go, he'll be there with me. I did all I could, not only to save my marriage, but also to save my husband's life. He told me to hold my head up, stand boldly, and watch his salvation." Ivy moved to the Queen Anne chair and sat down. "I've never seen the righteous forsaken nor his seed begging bread. If Ray has any other children, other than the ones we had together, I'm sure the Lord will provide."

"Yes, Ivy, the Lord will provide – and through you!" Anna said, dismissing Ivy's retort. "Now, I'm sure that brother of yours has already told you that Caroline is pregnant. So I'm sure my coming to you with this isn't a shock."

"Let me reiterate. I'm sure God will make a way for that child somehow. So you don't have to ask me about Caroline's baby again." Ivy stood. "As a matter of fact, my attorney will be handling all claims against Ray's estate. So I suggest you call Bill Hart."

"You always were a wiseass."

"Thank you. I'll take that as a compliment. Now, are we finished?"

"No. My son came here the other day for some of Ray's things. I'd like to get…"

"Nothing."

"I haven't even told you what I want."

"It doesn't matter. You will not come in my home and take anything at all."

"But…"

"And that's final." Ivy walked out of the room and into the entry hallway and stood at the front door. Anna followed her. "Now, if you'll excuse me, I have someplace I have to be."

Anna paused and appraised Ivy from head to toe, not moving to leave. "I have something else I need to discuss. It's… well… it's about my car."

Ivy saw that she was hesitant. "And what about it?

"My car was in Ray's name," she said as she dropped her head. "It's my understanding that he purchased a death policy that was being paid with the monthly car payment. And, when he passed, he assigned you as beneficiary. So, the car now belongs to you." Anna lifted her head to look at Ivy. "Ray stopped paying on that car some time ago, and I've been keeping up with the payments."

What Anna didn't know was that Ivy was the one that ordered that car a little over two years before, and had it delivered to her home after Ray told her that the engine in his mother's car had seized.

Ivy clasped her hands together and said, "I don't want your car, Mrs. Miller. That car was purchased for you. And, it's true; you've been paying the payments for over a year now. When the insurance company sends me the title, I'll be sure to forward it to you. Now," Ivy said opening the door wider, "if you don't mind, I'd like to get ready for my appointment."

As Anna walked to the door, she turned to Ivy and said, "Well, I'm sure you'll be at the reading of my son's will tomorrow."

"Yes, I'll be at the reading of my husband's will tomorrow," Ivy answered and then slammed the door behind her. Ivy was furious. She stood there with her eyes shut tightly to get her temper under control.

When she opened her eyes, Jade was standing in the hallway, her son in her arms. "You really handled her like a true Christian."

"I am so pissed!" Ivy said.

"Well, you know what the Bible says, be angry, just don't sin. I don't think you sinned in the least."

"There's also a scripture that says, parents, don't provoke your children to wrath."

"Oh, yeah, that's there too," Jade smiled. "Come on, let's go get brunch, 'cause breakfast is certainly over now."

"I'm not hungry."

"Don't even try it, Ivy. You were starving just before Anna came. Get your coat. We're going to IHop, and I don't want to have to drag you. So please, let's go." Ivy stood staring at her friend. "I mean it, Ivy. Don't make me act ugly in front of my son."

Ivy moved away from the door and brushed past Jade as she went in the closet for a coat. "You ain't bad," Ivy said as she threw Jade a look over her shoulder.

Jade burst out laughing and Ivy soon followed.

Chapter Sixteen

Sheena accompanied Ivy to the office of William K. Hart III, Esq.

Bill asked them to arrive an hour before the reading was to begin. When they arrived, Bill's secretary escorted them to Conference Room B where Bill was already waiting for them.

"Hi, Bill," Sheena greeted him, reaching out to shake his hand.

"Ladies," he said as he inclined his head. "How are you today?"

"We're fine, thank you," Sheena answered.

"You ladies can have a seat. Can I get you anything? Juice, coffee, water?"

"No, thank you." Sheena's voice got businesslike. "We're a little confused as to why you wanted Ivy to come in early."

Bill nodded. "Well, I have a doctor's report here. I thought you might want to see it before Ray's parents come. I think this record and statement from Ray's physician will make things go a lot smoother for Ivy."

"Bill, you should know that Anna came to see Ivy yesterday." Sheena still was using her attorney's voice.

"Yes, I know. Anna came here to see me yesterday as well, probably right after she left your house." Bill rested his head back onto his chair.

"Bill, I'd really rather not be here with Ray's parents. You know that," Ivy said.

"I know, but Ray wants everyone to be here at the same time when it's read. That was his request. Now, I can't make you stay…"

"No, if that's what he wanted, then I'll stay." Ivy dismissed the idea with a wave of her hand.

"Good. Now, I asked you to come early because I wanted you to look over the information I received from Ray's doctor." He handed Ivy the file. "I'm going into my office to make a phone call." Bill stood. "That will give you and Sheena a chance to look over his report."

"Okay, thanks," Sheena said.

Ivy and Sheena read the information in the file. According to the report, Ray was battling heart disease and with only thirty percent of his heart functioning, he was on the list for a transplant. "What in the world? Why didn't he tell me, Sheena?"

"I don't know. Maybe he didn't want you to worry. You already had your plate full, and the only thing I can think of why he didn't tell you is so you wouldn't worry about him.

"Now I'm more confused. Why would he tell me to divorce him?"

"I can answer that," Bill said as he walked back into the room and took his seat.

Ivy sat up in attention. *This I have to hear real good*, she said to herself.

Bill looked directly at Ivy. "He really didn't want a divorce. He told me that he probably wouldn't live to see the whole process through. Because he hadn't told me about his illness I thought it all had something to do with his drug use. I just figured he knew it had gotten worse so he was just changing his will and doing all that he was doing to simply protect you." He took a deep breath. "But Ray knew he was dying. So, now that I think about it, he wanted you to hate him so losing him later wouldn't hurt so badly. He knew that forcing you to give him a divorce would anger you and make you curse the day he was born. Then he said something that just didn't make sense to me until now. He said he didn't want you to be responsible for taking care of him if he ever became an invalid."

"But I would have!"

"Yes, and he knew that. But what you don't understand is that he was in an abyss so deep that he feared he'd drag you down in it with him. The health problems he was having were all because of the abuse he imposed on his body.

"Mr. Hart, the Millers are here," announced the secretary from the doorway.

"Give me a minute, Patty. They're early."

She nodded and walked away.

Ivy leaned back in the chair and took a deep breath to absorb what she had just read and what Bill had told her.

"You all right?" Sheena asked her.

"Yeah, I'm... I'm ... okay,' she stammered.

"Since they are here, we can go ahead with the reading. But if you need time to…"

"No, no. I want to get this over with," Ivy said.

"Okay, I'll be right back with the others."

Sheena leaned over to Ivy and asked, "Are you sure you're okay?"

Ivy looked up at her friend and said what she felt in her heart. "I really didn't know he truly loved me, Sheena, until this moment. The anxiety I was feeling just disappeared. It's gone." Sheena patted Ivy's hand, who choked up, close to tears.

The door opened and Ray's parents, sister, brother, and Caroline filed in taking up the seats at the other end of the long conference table, but Lisa came to sit next to Ivy.

"What are you doing, Lisa?" Anna asked her daughter.

Lisa leaned her head toward Ivy and put her hand on top of hers. "I don't approve, Ivy. I want you to know that."

Ivy knew she was talking about Caroline and her presence at the reading. She squeezed Lisa's hand and said, "I know. But don't make your mother upset with you because of me and…"

Lisa cut her off. "She's already upset with me. John and I are getting married."

Ivy smiled and turned in her seat to hug Lisa.

"Traitor," Anna blurted out.

Lisa did a quick grin at her mother. She was too in love and too happy to let her mother's attitude bring her down.

After everyone was assembled, Ivy sat motionless as Bill began to read the will.

Last Will And Testament of Raymond Miller

*I, **Raymond T. Miller**, a resident and citizen of Camden County, New Jersey, being of sound mind and disposing memory, do hereby make, publish, and declare this instrument to be my last will and testament, hereby revoking any and all wills and codicils by me at any time heretofore made*

*I direct my Executor, **Ivy Jones-Miller**, hereinafter named, to pay all of my matured debts and my funeral expenses, as well as the costs and expenses of the administration of my estate, as soon after my death as practicable. I further direct that all estate, inheritance, transfer, and succession taxes which are payable by reason under this will, be paid out of my residuary estate; and I hereby waive on behalf of my estate, any right to recover from any person any part of such taxes so paid. My Executor, in her sole discretion, may pay from my domiciliary estate all or any portion of the costs of ancillary administration and similar proceedings in other jurisdictions.*

I anticipate that included, as a part of my property and estate at the time of my death, will be tangible personal property of various kinds, characters, and values, including trophies and other items accumulated by me during my professional career. I, hereby, specifically instruct all concerned that my Executor, herein appointed, shall have complete freedom and discretion as to disposal of any and all such property in the best interest of my estate and my beneficiaries, and her discretion so exercised shall not be subject to question by anyone whomsoever.

As Bill read Ray's will aloud, Ivy felt Sheena tighten the grip on her hand. She closed her eyes tightly, absorbing what it all meant. Ray had left her everything that belonged to him, solely for her to dispose and keep at her own discretion, and he made it clear that he opposed anyone who challenged her. The will was short. It took less than three minutes to read. However, what was left to Ivy was enormous and unexpected.

For a few minutes after the will was read, the room was quiet. It seemed everyone was in shock.

Ray's father finally stood and asked, "So this means that everything that my son had belongs to his wife?"

"Yes, sir."

"It also means that the house we live in belongs to her too?"

"Yes, I'm afraid so."

"How can that be?" Peter asked. "That house was in both my parents' names. I saw the title myself."

"Yes it was, but your parents mortgaged the house seven years ago and they hadn't paid the taxes in three years. To keep the bank from taking the property, Ray purchased the mortgage, paid the taxes up-to-date, and then foreclosed on the property in his name. The house belongs to Ivy.

"Why wouldn't my son leave the house to me knowing we live there?" Mr. Miller asked.

"I know you had something to do with that," Anna said, looking directly at Ivy.

"Mrs. Miller, I do believe you're being unfair to your daughter-in-law. Ray changed his will less than two weeks before his death."

"Yes, but at that time, did he know she was divorcing him?" Anna asked.

"Yes, he knew."

"What about his child that isn't born to her?" Anna asked pointing to Ivy.

"If there is a child that was not named, then I'm sure the Executor of this will has no other choice but to consider its validity."

"Well, that's why Caroline is here. She's expecting a child in five months."

Bill looked at Caroline and asked her point-blank. "Is this true, Ms. Hall?"

"Yes," Caroline answered in a low voice.

"So it's true that the child you now carry belongs to the late Raymond T. Miller?"

"Yes," Caroline answered, her voice even lower.

Bill stared her down for a moment and then asked. "Are you sure? Because I have a statement from his doctor that tells me that Ray had a procedure performed on him that prevented him from fathering more children. And, that it was done only..." Bill flipped over a page in the folder in front of him "...one week after his wife gave birth to twins. And this report also indicates that Ray was told only six months ago that his heart was damaged due to his drug use and that he was in desperate need of a heart transplant. Furthermore, the medication that he was on made it impossible for him to perform sexually."

"My son was sick?" Mr. Miller asked.

"Your son was very ill indeed, according to his doctor. I didn't get this report until yesterday. And it shone a lot of light on Ray's behavior for the last few months." Bill turned his attention back to Caroline. "Now, we can do DNA testing. But you know as well as I do that the child you are carrying does not belong to Ray, isn't that right?"

Ray's mother turned her whole chair around to face Caroline who was sitting next to her. "Tell this man you are not a liar. Tell him that this child is my dead son's. Tell him." Caroline took a side look at Peter. "Tell him, girl. If a DNA test is what you want, then a DNA test you'll get."

"She can't," Ray's brother, Peter, blurted out.

"How would you know?"

"Because it's mine."

Ivy couldn't believe her ears, and Sheena gasped and then covered her mouth. Lisa was so mortified by what she just heard that she dropped her head in shame.

"What... How... When... Jesus, Pete!" Anna exclaimed.

Peter stood up. "Let's go, Caroline," he said as he directed his eyes across the table where she sat. Caroline stood.

"Why, Peter? What have I ever done to you to make you do something like this?" Ivy asked him.

"It's nothing against you, Ivy," Peter answered. "You're an innocent bystander when it comes to me and my brother. But since you asked why I did it, I'll tell you. It's because I knew a DNA test would be needed and I figured it wouldn't be a problem since Ray and I are brothers. But it all backfired cause he never told me he stopped himself from fathering more children and... he..." he turned to his mother and pointed at her from across the table.

"Come on, baby, let's go," Caroline pleaded now, standing next to him.

"No," Peter said in annoyance. "All this stuff between me and my brother is because of you, Mom. I wanted to be compensated for all the years of being second, even though I was the oldest."

"What are you talking about, boy? You're talking foolish. What you've done here is completely downright conniving and you're gonna blame me?" Anna asked.

"You never loved me like you did him. I was your son, too, but you never treated me like you did him. Never!" Peter said, raising his voice.

"That's not true. Why would you say this in front of these people? Why would you disgrace our family like this?" Anna asked as she waved her hand in front of her.

"Because, it's the truth, Anna," Carson said as he balled his hand into a fist and slammed it on the table. "And, I'm not covering for it anymore. Ain't no sense in it now that Ray's gone."

"Carson, we'll discuss this matter at home. Let's go," Anna said as she reached beside the chair to retrieve her purse.

"I'm sorry, Anna, but if I don't tell what needs to be told now, I'll probably never tell it."

"Have you lost your mind? I said, let's go."

Carson turned to Peter. "Anna's not your mother, son."

"Carson," Anna gasped. "Don't do this."

Peter froze where he stood and then slid down into the chair. Caroline sat in the chair next to him and gripped his hand.

"Do what, Anna? This should have been done years ago when I noticed you showing a difference in my sons."

"I'm not listening to this garbage. I'm leaving," Anna said with irritation.

"Goodbye," Carson said, shooting his wife a look.

All eyes were on the elderly couple. When Anna stood and didn't move to the door, Carson sarcastically asked, "What's the problem? You need some help to your car?"

Anna gave Carson a lethal look of her own. "No need for you to come home, 'cause you don't live there anymore."

"I believe we were just told we don't have a house anymore," Carson countered.

Anna jerked her body to the exit door. "I'm contesting this so-called will, Mr. Hart. So don't be surprised when my attorney contacts you."

Sheena leaned over and whispered to Ivy, "This is getting very interesting."

"I'll assure you, Mrs. Miller, this will is uncontestable. However, you have the right to try," Bill answered.

Anna sauntered out of the conference room, slamming the door behind her.

Peter was sitting in silence. Caroline looped her arm around his. He looked at his father and asked, "What are you saying to me?"

"I'm saying that you are my son, but not Anna's." Everyone's eyes were on Carson. He moved around in his chair trying to find comfort.

"So you finally decide to tell me now that my mother is not my mother."

"I was dating Anna when your mother got pregnant with you. I married Anna instead of her."

All the color seemed to drain from Peter's face. "I always knew, but I didn't want to believe it. Who's my mother?"

"It's not important who she was."

"Was?"

"You are my son. Anna really did the best she could under the circumstances."

Peter stood up, freeing his arm from Caroline's, and walked over to where his father was sitting. "I want to know right now who my mother is, Dad," he said between clinched teeth. "I'm thirty-four years old, and I have the right to know." Carson dropped his head. Everyone in the room was eager to know.

"Dad," Peter said, his voice low and burning. "It was Marilyn, right?

His father looked up at him in astonishment. "How... she told you?"

"Marilyn? Marilyn who?" Ivy thought.

As if Carson could hear her thoughts, he said, "Marilyn was Anna's first cousin. We moved here after she died."

"The same Marilyn that used to take me to spend weekends with her. The one I used to call May Lynn? She told me I was her son and to not let anyone know that she told me. She treated me like I was her son too. I should have known she wasn't a quack like Mom... no, Anna... said she was."

"Yeah, well, it's all my fault. I made a deal with her. I took custody of you from her and she was to see you on weekends. But after she died, I was free to move out of the state. That's when we moved next door to Ivy's family."

"Why, Dad?"

"We'll talk about all this at home. Let's go." Carson stood and looked over at Ivy. "I'm really sorry about all this, Ivy." Peter and Caroline eased out of the room first, without another word to anyone.

As Carson began to leave, Ivy called to him. "Mr. Miller." He turned to face Ivy. "Don't worry about the house. It's yours for as long as you live."

"Thank you, Ivy. But, I'm not going to live with Anna anymore. You take good care of yourself and my grandchildren. Once I get settled I'd like to get to know them."

Ivy nodded mutely.

Lisa stood. "I think it's best I leave, too," she said, then hugged both Ivy and Sheena.

Ivy stirred herself to speak. "I am so sorry about all of this."

"I am, too. I'll call you," Lisa said, holding her hand to her ear, simulating a phone.

After Lisa left the room, Sheena asked, "What in the world just happened in here?"

"Whew!" Bill blew out a sigh. "That's never happened to me in all the days I've been practicing law."

"That was pretty intense," Ivy remarked.

"I'm glad Ray did the right thing and left Ivy large and in charge," Sheena commented.

"Ray was far from being a fool," Bill said.

"Well, from what I see in this portfolio, he was worth over 1.5 million dollars."

"Actually, it's more," Bill said, as he leaned back, rocking his chair. "But when he came in to change the will he told me to make sure Ivy got everything, and to be sure it was uncontestable. He said, and I quote, "*She receives everything that I have, she's earned it.*"

"What did you mean when you said actually it was more?" Ivy asked in surprise.

"Well, you only see his NFL Pension, his IRA, and a few small bonds he had. But what you haven't taken in consideration are his two life insurance policies, and a few other things that couldn't be considered part of his financial status because they wouldn't take effect until he died. What I'm saying to you is he's worth more dead than alive."

"Two?" Sheena asked.

" Excuse me?" Bill asked.

"You said he had two insurance policies," Sheena said.

"Yes, he had two. One he took out in the middle of his career, and the other he took out about two years ago just before his career ended."

"I cashed that policy in to help pay for his drug treatment," Ivy said.

"No, that was another small policy he took out at the beginning of his career. He told me what you were trying to do for him and he told me not to tell you about the other policies. And, those policies where all doubled because he died by accident. One policy was a million and the younger one was five hundred thousand. Between the two policies, that's a total of three million."

Ivy looked at Bill. "I understand now why Ray kept me from you. He had a lot of secrets. So it wasn't that you disliked me. You just wanted to be loyal to your client."

Sheena looked at Bill and dropped her head.

"Yes, I have to be loyal to my clients," he said, purposely not giving himself away and letting her know his true feelings.

"Will you continue to do for me what you did for my husband?" When Bill didn't answer her right away, Ivy added, "Please, Bill. I trust you."

"Sure, Ivy. I'll... I'll continue to handle things for you."

"Thank you." Ivy stood and walked over to Bill's end of the table.

"You're welcome," Bill answered. "I'll be getting in touch with you about settling your estate. It will have to go to probate."

"I understand." Ivy stared at him a moment and then asked, "Can I hug you?" Bill smiled, stood up, and he gathered her in his arms. She stood on tiptoe as she kissed his cheek. "Thanks for being a friend," she said as she wiped her lipstick from his face with her thumb.

He smiled in appreciation.

Chapter Seventeen

Bill walked out of his office, soon after Sheena and Ivy, with the fragrance of Ivy's perfume and the feel of her soft lips on his cheek. *The contact was as innocent as it could be,* Bill thought as he stepped into the elevator that would take him to the tenth floor. *How in the world could such an innocent gesture as a hug and kiss on the cheek make me think about sharing the rest of my life with this woman?* Bill knew he was making it to be much more than it was. The elevator doors opened, and Bill stepped off to go to Marshall's office.

Bill approached the receptionist who was chatting on the phone. He waited until she finished her call. "Hi Pam."

"Hello, Mr. Hart."

"I have an appointment with Mr. Marshall. Is he here?"

"Yes, he's in. Have a seat. I'll let him know you're here."

"Thanks, Pam."

Bill sat down and reached for a magazine. He opened it and began to flip through it, though his mind was far from the pictures and printed words on the pages. For an instant, he closed his eyes and remembered that he just held the woman that haunted his dreams and made it impossible for him to have a meaning relationship with any other woman. His mind was running wild. *You're a sick puppy, Bill,* he told himself. *This woman just lost the love of her life. The only man she's ever loved. You know she's not thinking about you or any other man. So get a life.*

'Mr. Hart, Mr. Marshall will see you now."

"Thanks, Pam."

"Hey, Bill!"

"Marshall. You told me to see you right after I administered Ray's will."

"Yeah, I know I have what he left you right here."

Bill pushed a disk to the edge of his desk. "This DVD is for you. I recorded it for Ray the same day he changed his will. He told me to be sure you viewed this on the same day his will was read. Anyway, how did the reading go?"

"It had a surprise in it but I don't want to talk about that now. I want to know what's on the disk.

Bill made himself comfortable on the sofa while Marshall put the disk in the machine. Soon after it closed, Bill saw Ray's face and heard his voice.

"Are you ready?' Ray asked.

"It's recording now, Ray." He heard Marshall's voice in the background.

"Okay then. Well, hi, Bill. This is sad, isn't it? Me being dead and you losing such a wonderful client. So

let's have a moment of silence in remembrance of me."
Ray bowed his head. "Come on, man, bow your head
and give me some respect," Ray commanded.

Bill looked over at Marshall who had come to sit next
to him on the sofa. "Is he serious?"

"Keep watching and then you tell me if he's serious."

"Okay, enough," Ray said. "I just want you to know
that it's hard to talk about yourself like you're already
dead. But I've been working on this for about two
weeks now. I've asked myself that when I died who
would care for my family? Well, obviously, Ivy's father
and mother came to mind. They could handle my sons
for a while, but Dad is getting old. Besides, I need
someone who could take care of everyone, including
Ivy. And, that's where I need your help, Bill. You see,
man, I know you're in love with my wife."

"This is the part that tripped me," Marshall said.

"And she doesn't have a clue. Ivy's been sheltered,
first by her parents, then me. She's not street-wise at all
and she's a straight-up church girl and it ain't no act."

"How did he know?" Bill whispered.

"I know you're wondering how I know this. Well,
let's just say you can't hold your liquor, man. When
you told me why you didn't want my wife around you
and how she makes you feel, I started to punch you in
your mouth. But even drunk, you were respectful and
humble as you apologized for being in love with
another man's wife. I really appreciated the way your
drunken ass did it. And I kept my wife away from you.
I never wanted her to know how much more of a man
you are than me." Ray paused to look down at the paper
in his hand. "I knew you and Vincent Marshall here
were friends and that's why I chose him to give you this
message. So, since you already have feelings for Ivy, I
want you to take care of her... her and my... my

children." Ray paused and dropped his head. "I failed her. I should have listened to you and treated her like the queen she is. But since you're watching this video, it's too late for me now. I'm gone and you and her are still there. I'm going to help you out and cut about five years off your courtship. I want you to listen and listen good."

It took about forty-five minutes for Ray to give Bill the whole scoop on Ivy and each one of his children. At the end of his message he said, "My son Ray, he likes to fish, so you know those deep sea fishing trips you're always taking, well, take my son with you sometimes. I know Ivy would appreciate that, and it'll make Junior happy. I just want you to know that you have my blessing to pursue Ivy." Bill sat up on the edge of his seat. "I know you might find this recording shocking, but I was shocked when I realized I wasn't going to be here much longer. So whether it be my heart, or some other illness, or some freak accident; God gave me the chance to make right some of the wrong I've done. And I'm grateful." Bill's eyes were glued to the screen. "Oh, another thing. She thinks you don't care for her at all. She's asked me many times if she'd said or did anything to offend you. So if you haven't already told her that it's not anything that she has done or said, you need to handle that immediately. You've got your work cut out for you but I promise you, Ivy's worth it. Now, Marshall is gonna turn off this recording, 'cause I'm done with you." He looked down at his paper again and raising his head quickly he said, "Oh, I forgot, Ivy likes to do things proper. So, if you do something like maybe send her flowers for her birthday or take her and kids to the Philly Zoo, and she says to you don't do it because it isn't proper, then tell her being proper is being there for her anytime, anyplace, anywhere." Ray paused again. "Turn it off man." He looked in the camera and the screen turned blue.

"I'm speechless," Bill said.

"I figured you would be. He left a recording for Ivy too. And it's much deeper than yours. But, I'm only going to give it to her if you ask her to marry you and she refuses."

"What?"

"He said that you need to pop that question within two years."

"Look, man, I'm not letting a dead man manipulate me from the grave."

"Hey, call it what you want, but believe me he was sober and clear-headed when he made these videos. And I charged him."

"I'm sure you did," Bill said, shaking his head. "Can I get a copy of that?"

"No can do. He told me to allow you to see it once, and after that to destroy it."

Bill looked at Marshall, "Man, I won't…

"No, I can't do it. He told me why he wanted it destroyed and that's that. And don't ask me why, 'cause I'm not telling you."

* * *

A week later, Sheena sat with Ivy in her kitchen reviewing her copy of Ray's will again. Ray had left Ivy as the executor and Bill as the trustee. Sheena thought that ironic, forcing the two of them to work together in this way. Ivy had still been worried about debts and her financial future until she talked with a financial advisor yesterday. The advisor made it clear that she was totally free from debt for the rest of her life, as long she did what she told her to do with the bulk of her money.

Ivy instructed Sheena to do a quick claim deed on the house that Anna and Carson lived in.

"Ivy, if I were you…"

"But you're not me, Sheena. Ray left this in my hands because he knew I would do right by everyone. Just because his mother is a mean old battle-ax doesn't mean I shouldn't do what I feel in my heart to do. If she mortgages the house again, that's on her."

"Ivy, didn't Lisa tell you that her father has moved out of the house and is filing for a divorce?"

"She told me. So it will be up to a judge to sort out the mess, not me."

"Okay," Sheena said, throwing up her hands.

"Peter wanted Ray's clothes. Will you see that he gets them?"

"Okay."

Ivy looked down at the list she made. "Ray's father wants the collection of football cards they started when he was young. I want him to have them."

"You do know how much they're worth, right?" Sheena asked.

"Are you saying the cards are going to break me?"

"No, Ivy. I mean, did you ask Junior if he wanted them? He and Ray started collecting them too."

"Yes, I know, but he wants his grandfather to have them."

"Okay." Sheena threw her hands up again.

"Here," Ivy said as she pushed two sheets of paper to Sheena. "Just do what's on the list."

After reading the list, Sheena said, "You're crazy."

"I'm going to ask you what I asked Bill on yesterday. Is giving this stuff away going to risk my financial future?"

"It's not about the money, Ivy. Look what they did to you, how they tried to slander your name. Peter, of all people, and you're giving him the house in Florida?"

"Yes, I want him to have it. And, I'm giving *this house* to John and Lisa as a wedding gift."

"You know what? You've lost your mind."

"No, I haven't. I see things much clearer now. I talked it over with Bill yesterday. There are just too many memories here. So I'm going to move. Bill's going to find me a nice parcel of land, and I'm going to build a brand new house."

"I see. Okay."

"Sheena, don't worry about me. Bill has promised to work with me every step of the way. He has a friend that's an architect, and he's going to do my drawing as a favor to Bill."

"Oh, he has has he?"

"Yes, he is. And, don't be so pessimistic. He's being a good trustee to Ray's estate."

"Uh-huh."

"I'm serious."

"Oh, I'm serious too. Bill… he… well… he is a good man. " Sheena said, nodding her head.

"Yes, and I want to thank you too."

"For what?"

"For being my friend and loving me through the madness," Ivy said as she hugged her friend. "I didn't forget either that I owe you and the others some money for handling my bills last week."

"Well, now that you're loaded, you can give us back our money."

"Yeah, I told Bill that's exactly what I wanted to do." Ivy walked over to a stack of envelopes and pulled out three. "I was going to wait until Jade and Miranda got here, but I can give you yours first." Ivy handed one of the envelopes to Sheena. She stood where she was and opened it.

"No, Ivy. You can't do this."

"Yes, I can."

"Ivy no. I don't want it."

"I have one for each of you."

"Ivy, it's okay to pay me back, but to add a hundred thousand dollars to the figure is crazy."

"No, this money is a bribe."

"A bribe?"

"Yes, and a wedding gift."

"I'm not getting married."

"But you will. I'm sure you will someday. So the next time Jason asks you to marry him, think of this money as a bribe because I want some godchildren from you. You're getting old, girl, so you need to stop telling that man no."

"Oh, you got jokes."

Ivy laughed at Sheena. "Jade is so right about you."

"Really? What did she say this time, the miss know-it-all?"

Ivy laughed again.

* * *

Ivy, Sheena, Jade, and Miranda were all together later that evening, which happened to be the evening of the two-week anniversary of Ray's death.

Ivy wanted them to have the weekend they missed because of the tragedy, and she wanted to give each of them a gift of her appreciation.

They had been there over an hour just talking about old times. Sheena hadn't said a word about why Ivy had called them all together. So when Ivy stood and handed each of them an envelope and told them to open it, they were put off for a moment.

"I owe you guys. You were willing to help me when you thought I was busted and disgusted."

Jade's eyes widened when she saw the figure. "Ivy, you know you don't have to do this."

"I know I don't."

Miranda started to tear. "Ivy, I had so little to give."

"And?"

"Sheena and Jade are the ones who really put up the most cash. I can't take this."

"Randi, you gave what you had. And it was from your heart. So now, take what I have to give you from my heart."

Miranda truly did burst into tears.

"Well, I'm so glad you're doing this," Jade said happily. "Now, I can put a nice down payment on a house and…"

"Move your behind back to Jersey," Ivy completed her sentence.

"What?"

"You can move back home. This fall I want you back in law school. If you run out of money before you finish, come see me. I need attorneys to watch my attorneys," Ivy said, laughing. "So you can pack your stuff and move your behind back home. Dee needs a father and I need my godson," Ivy finished.

Sheena snickered at Jade.

"Oh, you find this humorous?"

"Very much so. My money is a bribe and a wedding gift."

Jade stared at Sheena for a moment, and then looked at Ivy bursting out in laughter. Shaking her head she said, "I was wondering how the Lord was going to make a way for me to finish law school. He sure works in mysterious ways."

"Yes, he does," Ivy admitted.

"So Sheena, when's the wedding?"

"I'm not marrying that man."

"By that man, she does mean Jason Jackson," Jade clarified.

"As always," Ivy answered. "But I'm letting her keep the money anyway. I never did approve of shot-gun weddings."

"I know what you mean," Jade said.

"Oh, I'm sure you do since, Ms Jade," Sheena said in a huff, "Jason and I don't have a child together."

"Oh, Sheena, please don't go there," Miranda pleaded.

"And, for all yall's information, Jason and I had a long talk in my office just today. We are friends and nothing more."

"Huh," Ivy grunted.

"Well, it's true. He told me he put in for a transfer and will probably be going to Atlanta or Raleigh in a few weeks, so that's that."

"You serious?" Ivy asked.

"Very," Sheena answered.

"And you're just gonna let him leave?" Ivy asked.

"What choice do I have? He's a grown man. I have no carte blanche on Jason," Sheena reasoned.

"No, but cupid has an arrow in his heart and it's yours," Jade said.

"I don't want to talk about it, so just let it go."

"What's Jason's number?" Jade asked getting up from her chair.

"Jade, let it go," Miranda warned.

"Sheena, this thing between you and Jason has gone far enough. The man told me himself that he's in love with you," Jade said.

"Oh yeah, well, Darrell told me he's in love with you. And, I don't see you running to the altar with his child in tow," Sheena answered.

"You… you all… you just don't understand. I'm in a different kind of dilemma," Jade stammered as she wiped her eyes.

"Please, enlighten us all, Jade, cause all of us are in the dark. And nobody can help you if you keep everything inside." Ivy said.

Jade sat back down in her chair. Shaking her head she said, "None of you will understand this. I'd rather keep those skeletons in my closet."

Ivy shrugged. "Okay. I think we need a group hug. These envelopes were made to put smiles on all your faces, and look at us!" Miranda joined Ivy on the floor first, then Sheena, and lastly Jade.

When the group broke up, Sheena and Jade held on to each other.

"You know I love you, you cow," Jade said to Sheena.

"Yeah I know, and I love you too, *Miss Know It All*."

Epilogue

18 Months Later

Adjusting to living without Ray had been rough in the beginning for Ivy and her four children. She spent many nights grieving his loss by crying herself to sleep. Thanks to Bill, she and the children were making a smooth transition.

Moving out of the house that she had shared with Ray helped tremendously. The new house was everything Ivy wanted it to be. No expense was spared to make it absolutely breathtaking. From the cathedral ceiling down to the hardwood floors, the house was a thing of beauty.

Like in her previous home, Ivy's favorite room was the kitchen. Here she sat looking out the glass panel walls, admiring her garden. She was proud and had every right to be. She planted her last rosebush earlier that day. Ivy couldn't wait to show it to Bill. He had thought the job would be too much for her to handle and offered to hire her a landscaper, but Ivy insisted on doing it herself.

Ivy turned her head to the kitchen entry when she heard one of her daughters call loudly, "Mommy, where are you?"

"I'm in here," she hollered out.

All four of her children raced into the kitchen, bursting with excitement.

"You missed it, Mom," Solomon said as he raced into the room and joined Ivy at the table where she was drinking sparkling apple cider. He picked up her glass and took a large gulp.

Tamara climbed on her mother's lap. "Look what Bill got me and Terra," she said stretching out her arm to show Ivy a beautiful charm bracelet.

"Oh, that's nice," Ivy gasped.

"I got one too, Mommy," Terra said, not to be outdone by her sister.

"Oh, yours is nice too."

"You missed it, Mom. You should of seen me slid down that giant water slid,' Solomon said, still excited. "It was awesome."

"Where did you all go?" Ivy asked.

"I took them to Clementon Lake Park," Bill answered.

"Yeah Mom, you missed it," Ray Junior said.

"Well, okay guys, remember what we talked about," Bill announced.

"Yeah," Terra said giggling.

"Okay then, let's get moving so you all can get cleaned up," Bill said.

The children quickly exited the room. Ivy stared at Bill, not saying one word. Bill sat down at the table and

Ivy continued to watch him. He picked up Ivy's glass, drained the rest of her cider, got up and went to the refrigerator. He pulled out the opened bottle of cider and emptied it into Ivy's glass. Bill sat down; Ivy was still staring at him.

After a few moments Bill asked, "What?"

"That's what I want to know," Ivy answered.

"I haven't the slightest idea what you're talking about."

"You're up to something, Bill Hart."

"Did you finish your garden masterpiece?"

Ivy's eyes lit up with delight. "Yes." She jumped up from her seat and headed to the back door. "Come on, let me show you."

"I'll look at it later because…"

"No," Ivy cried and moved to where he was sitting. Grabbing his hand, she pulled him. "Come on, Bill. I'm so proud of myself," she said, holding him by the hand and leading him through the door and out into the garden.

"Wow, it's beautiful!" Bill said in amazement.

"Yeah, man. And you said I couldn't do it."

"No, I never said you couldn't do it. I said it was a lot of work and you'd probably need some help."

"But I didn't need any help. And, look, the fountain is working perfectly," Ivy said.

"Yes, it is. Wow, I can't believe you did all this. The next time someone asks me about a landscaper, I'm gonna recommend you," Bill said as he began to walk over to the gazebo where the tulips were planted.

Ivy laughed. "Well, you make sure you let them know I'm expensive, but worth it."

Bill laughed as he sat down on the seat in the gazebo.

Ivy followed him and turned serious. "Bill, I need to talk to you."

"Yeah, about what?"

"About the kids and me... well... we've been monopolizing your time."

Bill shot her a look. "Have I complained?"

"No. But you should. Just a few weeks ago you were talking about how much you'd like to get married and have a family. But you're spending so much time with us that you don't have time to have a life of your own."

"Ivy, I like spending time with you and the kids."

"Yeah, but it's not proper."

"What?"

"Bill, just hear me out. Last week when we all went to Pizza Hut, a woman came in the restroom after me and said, *you have such beautiful children and they are so well mannered. My friend and I were just admiring your family.* At that moment, I realized that people think we're a couple."

"So?" Bill shrugged.

"Bill, I've been blocking you from other women, who..."

"You're not doing anything. I'm a grown man, Ivy. I choose to be with whom I want. I want to be with you and the kids."

"Will you please let me finish telling you the story?"

"Okay," he said stretching his arms out on the back of the seat.

Ivy sat down next to him on the seat. "I thanked the woman for the compliment and told her that they were my children, but you weren't my husband; but a very wonderful friend of mine."

"So that's why that woman kept staring at me while we were eating?"

"I didn't know anyone was staring at you."

"Yeah, well she was. I remember the woman that came out the restroom with you. I hate women who push up on men."

"Really, I didn't know that."

"I think there's a lot of things you don't know about me. For one, I don't be in places I don't want to be. Two, I love those kids in there," he said pointing to the house, "and three, I love you, Ivy."

Ivy smiled. "I love you too, Bill. But you need romance and I do too. Actually we're blocking each other."

"Oh, so that's what this is about," Bill said standing. "It's not about me, it's about you."

"Bill."

"Oh no. I get it. You want to date and I'm in the way. I see."

"No, that's not what I mean at all. You're twisting what I'm trying to say. Just let me explain."

"Okay, go ahead."

"I just think that we hog all your free time and we're getting too attached to you. You're here on Saturdays and all day Sunday. Last week you took the boys fishing, and today, on your day off, you took the kids to the amusement park."

"I do it…"

Ivy put her finger over his lips to stop him. "It's not just the kids Bill… it's me."

"Mom, Aunt Sheena is here," Ray Junior called.

"Sheena?" *Wonder what she's doing here*, she said to herself.

Bill had already stepped out of the gazebo and headed for the house. Ivy stepped into the door just moments after Bill.

"Thanks, Sheena." Bill said as he pushed something into his pants pocket.

Ivy heard Sheena ask her children, "You guys all ready?"

The children hollered, "Yeah."

"Good, so say goodbye to Bill and your mother. We need to put a move on, 'cause we don't want to be late."

"Late for what?" Ivy asked.

"Bill, you haven't talked to her?"

"I didn't get a chance."

"Well, you'll have the chance in a moment, 'cause we're out of here," Sheena said.

"Wait a minute. Where you goin' with my children?"

"Don't worry about where I'm going. You worry about where you're going since you don't have to worry with your crumb snatchers until tomorrow night," Sheena answered.

"Yeah, Mom. Have fun for once," Ray Junior said and then walked over to his mother and kissed her cheek. "Make sure she has lots of fun, okay?" He was looking at Bill.

Bill put his fist to the boy's cheek. "You know I will." Ray Junior smiled.

Ivy watched as Sheena took her children, leaving her and Bill alone. After Bill closed the door behind Sheena, he leaned against it and fixed his eyes on Ivy.

Ivy turned and walked into the kitchen, sitting in the seat she had vacated earlier. Picking up her glass of cider, she sipped it and asked, "What's going on, Bill?"

"Let's finish the conversation we had just before Sheena came," he said and sat next to her at the table.

"I don't want to talk about that anymore."

"Well, I do. Let me see where we left off. You said that you and the kids hog all my time."

"Well it's true and..."

Bill put his finger over her lips. "It's my turn to speak."

"But..."

"And then you said... let me see if I can remember correctly... you said, it's not just the kids, it's me."

Ivy stood up, "I'm not going to be interrogated by you."

"I'm not trying to interrogate you, baby."

Ivy looked at him. *He called me baby,* she thought.

"I'm just telling you what I told you earlier," Bill continued. "I love you, Ivy."

"I love you too, but..."

"No, you don't understand. I'm in love with you, baby. I don't want to be with anybody else. I don't want to date anybody else, and I don't want you seeing anybody else. I... love... you."

Ivy couldn't help that her eyes glassed up. She couldn't help but think that God had heard and answered her prayer. "You're in love with me?" She had to ask for confirmation.

"Yes, I'm in love with you. I know you care for me cause you and I really click, girl." Bill moved directly in front of Ivy and dropped to one knee.

Ivy gasped, knowing immediately what he was doing. He reached in his pocket and pulled out a burgundy box. He opened it as Ivy looked on. "Will you marry me?"

"Yes, yes." Ivy whispered.

Dear Reader:

I pray that you have enjoyed **IVY'S DILEMMA**. This book started out as a novel about four women each with a special dilemma. After working on it for two years, it became apparent that the novel was too long and complicated to be published all together in one book. So the Dilemma Series was born. **IVY'S DILEMMA** is the first to emerge from that long manuscript. I'm now putting the finishing touches on **JADE'S DILEMMA** who you met here in Ivy's story. In that book Jade will reveal all her hidden secrets and how they have affected her life and the choices she has made. You will also get a glimpse of Ivy again and see how she is progressing and the onset of **SHEENA'S DILEMMA**. I'm excited about these coming stories.

Please drop me a note and let me know your thoughts. Until next time, may God continue to bless and keep you, this is my prayer.

Peace,

Reign
P.O. Box 4731
Rocky Mount, NC 27803-0731

On the Web:
www.Reign.NickiAngela.net
Reign@NickiAngela.net

About The Author

Reign is the pseudonym used by an author who lives in North Carolina that works at a Housing Authority in a position that allows her to make a positive impact on the lives of others.

Reign lives with her husband and five of her six children.

Printed in the United States
68737LVS00001B/275

FEB 19 2007

9 780977 093601